FROM ASPHALT

J. E. PACE

Copyright © 2022 by Jean E. Knight Pace

All rights reserved.

No part of this book may be reproduced in any form or by any electronic or mechanical means, including information storage and retrieval systems, without written permission from the author, except for the use of brief quotations in a book review.

CHAPTER 1

LANCE

The front end of the semi is wrapped over the little gray Honda—tied up like a bow. They're lucky it wasn't a convertible, although it looks like one now, the top of the car sheared off by the semi's ride over it.

"People pay good money for an upgrade like that," I joke with my patient, who is miraculously still alive and even more miraculously still conscious. He's not in the mood for my stand-up though.

His shoulder and arm are torn and broken pretty severely in several places. I'm careful to use the technical words for the injury: laceration, fracture. I avoid words like 'shattered' and 'ripped.' He doesn't much appreciate these efforts either. Maybe he will in a few days or weeks; maybe not.

For now he's crying and asking about his wife, who is also alive, but not conscious. Truth be told, if you lined the two of them up side by side, his unconscious wife looks a lot better. On the outside. And that very detail is the thing that worries me most. I don't say any of that either.

"She's being taken care of," I say. Then, "Callen is one of the best paramedics I know." Also one of the newest. I leave that out too, because it also worries me. But Callen is sharp as a tack, and he hasn't lost a patient yet. A detail that also sort of worries me.

Each worry fighting its way toward my frontal cortex, each worry pushed down as I handle the most crucial problems at hand. Right now. In this moment.

This, after all, is a field of living in the moment—in the most non-zen way you can imagine. That's how crisis works. You fix the worst problem first, in any way you can, and then—if there's space and you've still got a living patient—you move on to the next moment.

In a way, it makes you appreciate the moments life grants you.

In another way, it makes you fear them.

The truck driver is shaken, but barely scratched. He waits to the side, a police officer asking him questions. More details that fly out of my head as quickly as they come into it.

Me? I get my patient on the backboard, cut off his shirt, or the parts of it that aren't jammed into wounds, bandage up the places that are bleeding the worst, then an IV to pump him up with Fentanyl—which he's really going to appreciate in a minute.

Callen and a volunteer firefighter are loading the stretcher with the guy's wife into our ambulance. Another ambulance is coming for me and my patient, but Callen will have to wait till it gets here to go.

We can hear the sirens from the other ambulance as it approaches. The firefighter heads to the front of the ambulance to drive.

It's then that I see it—a little animal limping along the side of the road. A mutt who seems to have a piece of debris stuck in its leg.

It's also then that Callen's patient codes. "Lance!" he shouts, though I'm already moving. I get my patient to the other ambulance and give them a quick rundown. Then hop into the back of Callen's ambulance. Callen and I start to bag his patient, check her heart rhythm, and pump her up with epinephrine.

Somewhere in a place that seems far away, her husband wails as the other unit loads him into his own ambulance. We're doing chest compressions as the volunteer firefighter takes the wheel. And then we drive drive drive, my adrenaline eating up the sound of the sirens, blurring the other cars on my road. We get to the hospital in less than four minutes.

Doctors and nurses rush out, and we rush the patients in.

And then we're done.

It used to be a bit of a high—back when I started six years ago; it isn't any more. Maybe I'm a little like a drug addict—so accustomed to the chemical hit that happens when things get tense that I don't notice it anymore. Or maybe I'm just some kind of sociopath who's gone numb to the feeling entirely.

Either way, after the call, I do my paperwork, glad that Callen had the patient who coded, not me. When the paperwork is done, the details start to drain from my memory. Not quite all the way, not yet, but they begin.

Later, I might remember a face, the color of a shirt, the treatment of a specific injury, but a year from now it'll be hard to recall a lot of the particulars of this call.

Call me callous if you want, but we've got to survive. If we held onto every single detail of every deadly call that crossed our paths, we'd be holding a lot. And honestly, we already do.

At this moment, all I can think of is the little dog on scene, limping along the asphalt—dark brown, sleek floppy ears, tufts of shaggy fur around its neck and knees, one paw held tight to its chest.

Had it been in one of the vehicles? Or was it just an innocent bystander caught in the crossfire? For all I know, it was just a stray who got its paw hurt years ago and has been scrapping along since then. Either way, I figure I'll never find out more. I've got five more hours of my shift and then a ten-minute ride to my condo for some sweet, sweet sleep before the next night's shift starts again.

Except that our final call goes over. By nearly an hour. It's out in the country and the guy is dead when we arrive, which means we have to wait for the coroner.

It seems like getting back to the station an hour late would send me racing home all the faster. But Callen wants to talk. An occurrence that's unusual enough that I stay after, sitting in his car for an extra forty-five minutes. Patients who code after trauma almost never make it. I know it, and Callen knows it.

"Go get some sleep," I tell him.

But then, I can't. I head home, strip down, roll around in my bed.

Around noon, I climb back out and figure I'll go get some lunch someplace. Except I don't. I go back to the scene, back to the place where my patient shattered and Callen's patient coded and I saw a dog limping around.

Bits of broken glass still sparkle here and there in the sun. I don't really expect to see the dog.

Until it limps in front of my car like it's on some kind of suicide mission.

I slam on the brakes and it scampers off into the thin line of woods at the side of the road. I pull over, park on the shoulder, and call out for it. No response. I'm scanning the line of trees, looking for movement, when I remember the bag of jerky I keep under my seat.

That does the trick.

In seconds the animal is at my side, chomping away. No collar or tags. I scoop it up off the asphalt and into a box that I'd put into my car.

If someone had asked me why I put that box into my car, I would have shrugged. Over the years you just learn to trust your instincts. And that box was calling to mine. Why a box? Because dogs pee, especially little distressed ones, and I just paid off my car.

My instinct was right about the dog too. She has a little shard of metal jutting out of her front paw. Not only that, but even though she's young, one of her eyes is a bit foggy. I'd guess she's blind in it, which might explain the running in front of things.

Once we're settled into my car, I try to get a better look at her leg. Which doesn't go well. Each time I come near it, a growl rises up in her throat, and the one time I manage to touch it, she snaps, almost biting me. Turns out dogs with metal stuck in their legs aren't that much different than people with metal stuck in their bodies. Only this time, I can't give a dose of anesthetic. Instead I stick another piece of jerky in the box. Since I can't drug the dog, I'm going to have to go somewhere where they can.

"You ready for a joyride with a stranger?" I ask her, googling the nearest vet clinic.

She looks very ready, even eager, for the joy ride, despite her hurt leg and the total stranger at her side.

"Alright," I say, strapping the box up with the seat belt. "Let's see if they've got an opening."

They do.

I'm lucky enough to have the good news delivered to me by one of the prettiest women I've ever seen in my life. Red curls tucked up into a loose bun, creamy skin like she belonged on an infomercial. Her lips are tucked away behind a mask, though I find that I kind of enjoy imagining them.

At this point I'm working on just a few hours of broken sleep, and this assistant is giving me something pleasant to do. I should thank her. When she glances up at me, I see that her eyes are blue—a sky you could fall into. Man, I really need some sleep, but looking at the clipboard in her hands, I begin to doubt I'll be getting any.

How long have I owned the dog? What is the dog's name? How did this happen?

Simple questions for someone who actually owns their own dog; much more difficult for me. If I'd thought about it for a minute, the obvious choice would have been to say, "I just saw her on the road and could tell she needed help." Good Samaritan style.

What I actually do is make up an elaborate history for me and this dog who, as far as I know, currently has some little seven-year-old owner posting signs all over town about how little Froofy is missing.

I don't name her Froofy though.

"Maverick," I say when the assistant asks for her name. "But I just call her Mavvy." I wink.

She smiles back—a through-the-mask smile that barely crinkles at the eyes. Then she glances back at the clipboard.

"And your name, sir?"

"Oh, Lance Patterson."

"How'd this happen?"

"I don't actually know," I say. Maybe the first truth of the day. "She ran off and when I found her, she was wandering by the side of the road with this chunk of metal in her leg." I look down. "I heard there was a wreck earlier and I wonder if something happened then."

She responds to my theory with another question. "When was the wreck?"

I have to resist the urge to say, "1:22 a.m." And just answer, "Sometime early this morning."

For a moment the clipboard comes down. "I'm glad you found her. But if not, someone probably would have brought her in and we could have checked her chip and called you."

She pulls the mask down, and smiles for real this time. It's only then that I realize all her other looks have been for politeness' sake.

I clear my throat, like the guilt just ran down and got stuck there. Maverick and I may have only a very brief and embarrassing history together. "Chip?" I ask.

"Yeah," she says. "The one they implanted when she was fixed. Speaking of," she continues. "How long ago was that?"

Suddenly I don't care so much what color this girl's eyes are, or even what her lips look like. "I don't really remember," I say.

"Well, we'll check the chip when we get her in for you."

I feel my stomach lurch. "Great, okay," I say. And now is also the time to come clean, to say something like, *To be honest, I just found this dog and wanted to help her. I thought that afterwards I would try to find her home and didn't realize it was more complicated than that.*

But I don't want to field any more questions from the assistant with her rosy cheeks. She's leaning down toward Maverick, who growls when she comes near the paw.

"Oh wow," the redhead says. "Poor girl." She touches Maverick on the back and the dog allows it. A little buzzer beeps and she looks back at me. "Come on back. Dr. Reynolds is ready for her."

I'm not really a natural liar (which is what the best liars probably say), and I almost gush out the whole story, but the woman has lifted the box—box, not carrier. I realize in a rush that the assistant probably noticed that right at the beginning.

She turns to me as we enter the room, another smile, though we're back to politeness.

I steal a quick glance at her nametag. Rebecca. I like the swoop of it.

Too bad I'll never be able to see her, or face her, again.

CHAPTER 2

Another guy. Another lie. Through his teeth. I have no idea how he got that dog, but it's not his.

Lucky for me, one lie deserves another. If he asks, and I kind of expect him to ask, I'll tell him I have a boyfriend. If I was gutsier, I'd tell him I have a boyfriend who isn't a liar, but I have a feeling that Dr. Reynolds wouldn't appreciate that with the customers. After all, they're not paying for me to harass them, no matter how obnoxious they are. And trust me, pet moms and dads can be really obnoxious.

Sometimes I think they just hired me because of my absolute cuteness. That's right. I'm adorable. It's my thing—the thing I do best. Which isn't a brag. I don't want it to be the thing I do best. It's not that I hate being cute. Not exactly. It's just that I want to be *not only* cute.

I bounce around Swallowsville College's website, thinking of that guy Mance or Chance or whatever his name is. If he wasn't a liar, he might be a decent catch. For someone. I click on the next class to distract myself. Algebra I.

I maybe wouldn't ever have to think of that guy again if it wasn't for the fact that the poor dog has to go in for surgery. Which means what's-his-name will be back tomorrow, if he bothers to come. Goody.

I click away from Algebra. I'll only take it if I need to for this imaginary major I haven't figured out. My phone buzzes. Sally Mae, my sister.

I let it ring through, glancing through math classes and wondering where I should propel my life. When I'm way past the age I should have it all figured out, and definitely older than a traditional college kid. Almost thirty-one.

My sister keeps telling me to do zoology and then go to veterinarian school. It does feel like the natural fit. I love animals—all of them, love them like crazy. I guess I'd have to since I work at a vet clinic, but it's more than that—we've got animal-loving genes in the family. My sister herself is the animal queen—hosting a successful YouTube channel with inspiring stories.

But. There's always a but.

I just don't want to be a veterinarian. I don't want to put animals to sleep or set animal bones or shove animal guts back in after they've been hit by a car, and did I mention putting them to sleep. Also, the richer your clientele gets, the crazier they become. And the poorer they get, the rougher things become —barking, biting dogs; barking, biting humans. Neither is my favorite situation.

Because sometimes my cuteness just hits a wall. I mean, not on the outside. I'm pretty good at keeping it glued on there, but inside it just takes a few mean words before my internal sweetness melts away.

I scroll through the listings at the local college. World lit. Art history. Mechanics. Computer programming. Culinary arts. There are hundreds.

It feels a little like online dating. Which was "the one"—that right first class for me? I don't want to be a vet. I'm not super interested in the arts or the humanities. History? No thanks. I don't want to work in marketing or business or tech, even though I'm pretty decent at those things. And I don't want to fight my way into the service industry, the fashion industry, or the entertainment industry.

What does that leave for somebody as stereotypically darling as myself? After all, my sister's already got the YouTube channel. Oh, and don't let that fool you. Those YouTubers might look sweet as candy on screen, but to make it on the internet, you have to be a Girl Boss supreme. And she is. In all the best ways, and a few not-so-best ways (which is why it's a secret still that I don't want to go to veterinarian school—she's just so intense about it, so positive that it will be the very best thing for me). Trouble is, I'm not sure. Not even a little.

I click on a chemistry class, imagine combining chemicals and blowing things up. Girl Boss style. Or crazy scientist style. There's a definite appeal to the idea. I buzz through some of the other sciences, which all sound kind of interesting. I pause on zoology, read the description for the millionth time, then glance at the clock.

Time to stop thinking about what class to "date" and to get ready for my actual date. Another guy my sister has hooked me up with.

And in case you're asking, no, I can't say no, at least not to Sally Mae (told you; she's a total Girl Boss). Besides, the last time she fixed me up with someone, things worked out pretty well. Not with the guy—he wound up with another girlfriend. But that girlfriend also wound up as one of my best friends. So...win-win, because dating Tad would have felt like dating my brother, no matter how good-looking he is. Truthfully, he's a lot happier with Macie than he would have been with me—wandering, adorable me.

I click away from zoology, back to the chem description. It sounds hard. My sister rocked her way through high school, then college, then started a successful YouTube channel in a world where people said you couldn't. I wobbled my way through high school, did a semester of college before doing a string of other jobs, finally settling on my current one. And now here I am looking at night classes. I shut the laptop, frustrated with myself, and dig out the new outfit I bought, along with a pretty coral lipstick. Cuteness, here I come.

This guy shows up with roses and then takes me to dinner. I'm not sure if there are strings attached to all the affection. He's good-looking, a doctor, interesting to talk to, and...newly single. That's not an inherent problem; my friend, Macie, is divorced too. But it's the kind of detail that makes me nervous, especially since I'm ten years younger than he is. Age difference aside, I'm old enough to know when a guy is looking for cute. And this guy is definitely looking for cute.

I leave him at my doorstep—1950s style. And when I do, I doubt he'll call again. After all, cute thirty-somethings are a dime a dozen; a surgeon shouldn't have to work too hard to find himself one. Which is why I'm kind of over being one. Not a feminist hippy enough to shave my head and join the Peace Corps and do whatever those tough girls do, but I can't help thinking that there's something I should do, something more "me" than just a few blind dates and a day job as an assistant for an animal doctor.

BECCA

The little dog, Maverick, or whatever her real name is, is coming out of anesthesia and she's just the cutest thing. Super soft ears that I stroke as she comes to, sniffing and drooling, then trying to stand on wobbly legs.

"Hang on, darlin'," I say, patting her back, then pulling a long silky ear through my fingers again. She settles down, plunking her side rump onto my hand and not knowing it. I kind of giggle, not realizing the vet is standing behind me.

"How's she doing?" Dr. Reynolds asks, and I startle.

"She's precious." I pull my hand out from her sleepy body and fill in my paperwork.

"Aren't they all?" she answers, interrupting my reading.

"No," I say. And we both laugh. I glance at Maverick's paperwork. She's probably just over a year old, judging from her teeth, a couple of which are broken. They'll need to be pulled.

"Oh, the animals aren't so bad," Dr. Reynolds replies.

Which reminds me. "Did you check the chip by any chance?"

Dr. Reynolds glances sideways at me. "Why do you ask?"

I shrug as innocently as I can manage, but Reynolds is not easily fooled by cuteness.

"Just curious," I say.

"I did not check it," Reynolds says. "Because there wasn't one. I guess Mr. Patterson must have not gotten around to having one inserted."

I pop an eyebrow. "Surprising that the last vet he took her to didn't insist. A vet that wasn't us, by the way."

"The dog is clearly a stray," she answers, reaching over to pet the sleepy dog. "As you well know. I think he must have found her recently. And picking up strays is allowed."

"Did you catch her up with her shots?"

Dr. Reynolds nods to the clipboard. "I gave her the first round. She'd also benefit from having three more teeth pulled, though I did the two most damaged today. I called Mr. Patterson and he gave me the go ahead. The guy's clearly got skin in the game."

I look at Maverick's little paw, all bandaged up. I feel a slight softening about Lance Patterson fibbing until I have an epiphany: He probably hit the dog—maybe with the side of his car, maybe with a bit of debris from the road. This is a guilt-trip thing. Otherwise, why not take the dog to the humane society?

I don't share my theory with Dr. Reynolds, mostly because I'm not at all in the mood for arguing, but it's one of those things I feel deep down in my bones. He hurt the dog, accidentally sure, then brought her here. "Oh Maverick," I murmur. "What have you gotten yourself into?"

Reynolds taps at a figure at the bottom of the clipboard and I suck in a breath. Over a thousand bucks. You could get a really nice breed for that price. This guy got himself a slightly gimpy mutt, a gimpy mutt with a wacky eye. You can't exactly hate a guy like that, even if he does tell lies, even if he's likely the one responsible for her injury in the first place.

"And her eye?" I ask, looking at the foggy one.

"Pretty sure she was born with it, and I don't think there's anything I can do. She's blind or partially blind. If he wanted to fix it, he'd need to find an expert and that…" She rubs her fingers together, making the money sign.

"I'll get the carrier," I say.

"You mean the cardboard box," Reynolds laughs. "Give him one of the official cardboard boxes at least." She nods to a stack in the corner—boxes we sometimes use when people come in without carriers. "I won't even charge him the five bucks for it. Good Samaritan that he is."

I open my mouth, almost mentioning my theory about the injury, but what's the point. This guy will be here today, then gone. My stomach clamps up a little on the thought when I look at sweet Maverick with her velvet ears and newly shaved leg. "Good as new, aren't you, sweetheart?" I say, setting the makeshift carrier on the table beside her before heading out to the lobby to find her savior, that liar.

He's the only one in the waiting room, sitting in a chair and fidgeting like it's his wife, not a stray dog, who's been in surgery. "How's she been?" he asks, standing up (I won't quite say 'leaping up,' but it was in that zone).

"She came through like a champ. Dr. Reynolds has her all stitched up. I'll take you back and you can have a look."

My cuteness is on full force, or maybe full guard. I want to lean over and say something like, "I know what you did to that dog," but I manage to restrain myself behind a bright smile—a smile that has gotten me countless phone numbers and zero boyfriends.

Lance lets out an audible sigh of relief when he sees her. The doctor is holding the clipboard and I'm holding my breath. I hope Dr. Reynolds gave him the skinny about the price over the phone, because it's never fun to hand over the bill.

"We've got her ready to go home," Dr. Reynolds says. "She'll need plenty of fluids, some sleep, and food. If she hasn't eaten within twenty-four hours, give us a call."

"Any food you recommend for a recovering dog?" he asks, and I can hear it again—the lie in his voice. He doesn't even know what to feed her.

"Whatever her normal food is should do. Her mouth might be a little tender from the tooth extractions, so you should soak hard food in water before feeding it to her."

He looks a little miserable and Dr. Reynolds takes pity on him. "PureNature is my favorite brand. Soaks well too."

The guy's face clears a little till he glances at that bill and swallows. But he doesn't blow up or freak out. Reynolds must have prepped him on the phone. All he does is lean down and murmur, "You cost more than a girlfriend."

Reynolds kind of laughs. "And she's just getting started. She'll need another round of shots in a couple months. If you decide to do those teeth, let me know. We don't want them to rot or get infected. If you bring her on a Wednesday, I'll give you a discount."

"Wow, that'd be great," he says. "Why Wednesday?"

"It's our slowest day," I answer.

Doctor Reynolds shows him Maverick's foot, and hands him a packet with fresh bandages, a tube of antibiotic, and a small pill in case she starts to show signs of significant pain. "Just mix it into some pudding," she says. "Soft foods for the next few days; check the gums for signs of infection. Here's the medicine for her mouth. And I think you're good to go. Oops, almost forgot," she says, when I hand her the cone. Dr. Reynolds shows him how to put it on.

I lift Maverick into her box carrier, stroking that ear one final time. "You were a good girl," I whisper, then walk with the pet dad out to the lobby.

"Thanks," he says as we walk toward the door.

"What happened anyway?" I ask suddenly. It's not a question I would have asked any other pet parent, no matter how odd the injury.

"I just found her, and she was hurt."

"Yeah," I murmur. "Poor thing." I look at him, trying to work the cute out of my eyes, trying to tell him I mean business and he better not be a jerk to that dog.

"Truth be told," he answers, looking down, "I think it happened in a car accident." He grabs the carrier and bolts out the door.

But at least there was that. At least he fessed up just a little.

"You really would be a great vet," Dr. Reynolds says as I clean the table.

"Yeah, maybe," I say.

She laughs. "Oh, I know it's not what you want long term. I just want you to know you really would be good at it."

I barely hear the compliment. How did she know it wasn't what I wanted? I'm sweet to all the animals, all the pet parents. "What do you mean?" I catch myself asking. "That it's not what I want."

She looks over her glasses at me. "You're just…" she begins, "…not always here. Your head is somewhere else. Today was the most I've seen you engage with an animal in weeks."

"She was cute," I defend myself (against the compliment).

"They're all cute," Reynolds answers.

"Yeah, I guess," I mutter.

"My point exactly. They're all cute to me and they get my attention, and I love it when I can fix them, when all I have to do is extract a nasty shard of metal from a leg."

I nod. "My sister keeps trying to convert me to veterinary school. That, or YouTube. She says she can hire me to edit or write interview questions or something. She'll pay me."

"Are you going to do it?" Reynolds asks, looking down at her laptop and making a note.

I smile, my cutest one. Being the little sister of a Girl Boss is tough enough. Working for her, uh-uh. "I think I'm happier with you," I say honestly.

"Well, I'm flattered. And thanks for getting that done so quickly. We've got Mrs. Pemberly at ten."

Inside I groan. Mrs. Pemberly. Seventy-thousand years old with a pet for every year. She smells like she just disinfected with old boots, and always talks with spittle. Her cats aren't much better. But the groan stays in and on the outside I grin. "I'll get her."

She's waiting with two cats in the same carrier. I swear one looks pregnant and suddenly I realize that this is what she probably considers a "married" pair. And in we go.

CHAPTER 4

LANCE

That girl. Woman. Probably early thirties, same as me. But there's something so girlish about her. Except for those eyes eyes eyes. Why did I tell her the dog might have been in a car accident? Truthfully, I don't even remember my original story, but I know this—those eyes are onto me, even when the smile looks innocent.

I help Maverick from the box, which is only a little different than the box I used, in that it has a handle.

She totters around, then flops on the floor, her ears settling last.

"We've got to get you some food."

I might as well have said. "We've got to get you some dirt," for all the enthusiasm she shows, but I bought PureNature on the way home. It cost nearly twenty-five dollars and by golly we are going to use it. Water into one of my cereal bowls, a little food tossed in. But she's not into food; she's standing by the door, staring out. Even I know what that means. "You gotta go?" I ask.

She wiggles her bum. But I've got no fence, no leash. Hopefully there's not some HOA thing about pets. "I just paid $1050 bucks," I tell her. "Don't run off."

Lucky for me, she's too drugged still. She does her business, then wobbles around. I pick her up and carry her inside, setting her next to the food. She flops down again. "Eat," I say. "Drink." I get another cereal bowl, fill it only with water. Nothing works. She just sleeps.

I shake her awake after an hour, trying to get her to eat again. She falls asleep with one ear in the dish. I move it out, pat it dry, then go to make myself a BLT for my own dinner. As soon as I'm seated, she pops open an eye. Then another. Lifts her bum, and limps over. "This is mine," I say. "You've got yours."

She disagrees.

And soon she's eaten most of the bacon as well as my crusts with a bit of bacon grease for dessert.

Afterwards she limps to the clean water and helps herself.

"You rat," I mutter, finishing off my last bite. I don't personally want bacon grease for dessert and scrounge up a bag of chocolate chips instead.

Just before bed, I get a call from the other paramedic, Callen. "She died, man." He's not one to beat around the bush.

"Who?" I say, though I have a pretty good idea.

"That lady, the one we worked. On that bad wreck."

It's not a surprise. It's never a surprise in a field where things have gone downhill long before you got there. It's just that every once in a while I want a surprise. Every once in a while, I want things to go right, to be right instead of ending up all wrong.

I keep thinking of her husband—trying to look over at her, trying to get to her. "She hasn't even opened her present." That's what he kept saying to me, to the point that I was starting to wonder if he'd gotten a little damage to his brain. Until I finally asked, "What present?"

"It's our thirtieth wedding anniversary," he answered, and then I looked down, noticed the suit jacket we'd thrown to the side, the nice fabric of the shirt I'd just cut through, the silver cuff links still on one wrist.

"She'll be okay," I'd said then. A total lie. What I should have said, what would have been true was, "We'll do our best." That's something I can say, something that has meaning. And maybe he sensed that lack of meaning because after that he stopped asking how she was, as though he knew that when people start making promises, they've got to be lying.

And I had been.

"I'm so sorry, dude," I say to Callen.

"Yeah, no biggie," he answers. "It's how it goes, right?"

We're all liars, I realize. Telling ourselves that everything's cool even as we pick up the phone to call someone else so that they can tell you that sure, everything's cool. This is just how things go; it's just how life is. At least on the calls. Not in regular life, of course. Not in your life. No, in those places, people don't die suddenly. Disasters don't take them—disasters that you have all of zero control over. That's a thing for work; that's what we promise one another. Work, not life.

"Definitely how it goes," I reply. "Don't worry; we'll save the next one."

Another lie. Even worse than the last. Statistically we save almost no one. Not when they're that far gone. Sure, we can help a diabetic whose sugar has gotten low. Sure, we can help with wounds or bleeding. But when a person codes after a traumatic crash, it's not looking much like a life we'll save. Oh, sometimes it is, sure. Otherwise, we'd probably never do it at all—never make ourselves that promise that the sirens and speed tempt us to make—that this time will be different, that if you're doing all you can, the person will come back, live their life, get the present her husband bought for her.

I realize that Callen hasn't answered me, that he's just breathing into the phone, like he's trying to keep his emotions together.

"We'll get the next one," I repeat.

"Yeah," he says, his breath evening out. "Good talking to you, man."

And the phone call ends.

I wander through my condo, like I don't know where I'm going. I pick up my toothbrush and set it down. Boil water for what, I don't know. Not dinner at this time of night, and I don't own a tea bag. Maverick trot-limps after me, stopping at each irrational place I stop.

Finally I settle in the bathroom, shave my face. She looks up at me through her cone, the injured leg lifted slightly off the floor.

"Time for bed, little girl," I say.

She whimpers.

I bend over and pick her up, tucking her against my chest and holding her good paw, like we're holding hands. Because sometimes you need a hand to hold. It's then I notice that in her good paw, there's a little burr stuck in the fur, probably from my yard. I wonder how many are in there.

"Ouch," I say to her, setting her on the bathmat and teasing open her little toes, the movements of my hands uncommonly slow. I'm grateful for the distraction, for this thing to focus on. This isn't the work of saving lives. It's more like taking out splinters, or playing the game Operation. Slow, steady, meticulous. Everything I'm normally not. I tease out the bit of thistle, far enough to grab it with the tweezers and pull. She whimpers. "Hey, girl," I say. "I know it's not fun, but we've got to do it. Otherwise, it'll hurt you more."

She looks into my eyes with her good eye and her

foggy one—neither eye believing me. Do I blame her? I tease open the next toe to see if she's got more, and she snaps at my hand. Not with full commitment, and the cone gets in the way, but there's definitely a couple more burrs tangled in those tufts of fur between her toes.

"Don't make me muzzle you," I threaten, though I'm all talk. I haven't even bought a leash; muzzles seem way out of my league.

I slow my movements even more. This time when I get to the part where I could have used the tweezers, I continue to massage the little bit of burr out and away. It feels impossible—moving each little piece of hair off of each sticky bit of burr. The minutes melt together, the movements taking on a little meditation of their own. And then, I look down and the burr is in my hand. Maverick hasn't so much as jerked.

"Let's just check those other toes," I say. But she's not listening. She's laid her head on the ground and is almost beginning to snore.

I touch the next bristly hitchhiker with my forefinger. I can't even feel the sticky burrs, only the tiny mound under the mop that is her toe fur. This one is deep. I part the hairs, almost tenderly now, until that first miniature spike pokes out—truth under all those layers—truth, making itself known.

I need to call Callen back, and I know it. Need to tell him that it is okay, but only because sometimes it's not, and that's okay too.

"Thanks, girl," I murmur to Maverick. She doesn't move, but makes a little cooing sound in her sleep.

Maverick's first night with me. She's bacon-fed and burr-free. What more can she ask for? I'm planning to leave her in the bathroom with a bowl of water. I'm mentally prepared for howling, for scratching, for bad behavior. What I'm not mentally ready for is the pitiful crying that ensues—she sounds almost like a human baby.

I go in, pet her to sleep, return to bed. And the crying starts again. I'm used to long, odd hours at work, but this is supposed to be my night off.

I gather her up in my arms, careful to avoid the wounded leg, then lay her in bed beside me. I take off her cone and both of us are asleep in minutes.

I wake up at dawn with a soft ear covering my

chest, and then she lets out a day-old-bacon-grease fart, and I jump out of bed, trying to wave away the scent before hurrying her out the door to do her business. The sun isn't quite out yet.

This time she lingers and stalls and I have to come after her. She tries to limp off, but her bad leg slows her enough that I can catch her before she's gone too far. Still, it's clear that I'm going to need some type of leash—something to keep her in the backyard and maybe something else to take her for walks once the leg is recovered.

She still turns her nose up at the soggy food I offer and only laps messily at her water for a second. Then it's back to bed. Or at least she tries to go back to bed. She can't quite make the jump. She stands at the side, the bad leg up against her chest, looking droopy and tired with her head hanging down. That cloudy eye and the clear one. She pushes her nose against the sheet. I squat in front of her, put an arm out. She puts a paw against it. She doesn't scratch or even really paw at me; she just…holds my hand.

"Fine," I say, lifting her into bed, then crawling back in myself. "You fart like that again, though, and I'm locking you out of the room and putting my noise cancelling headphones on."

She doesn't bother with an answer, or even a

look, just curls into a ball on the other side of the bed—the side that, ideally, would one day hold a woman.

I dust away that thought and burrow my own body back into the blankets. She lifts her head, tips it up at me. Then lifts her body with a bit of an effort, shaking out of the circle of a spot she'd just made for herself.

She hobbles over to me, noses at the blankets, digging into them. And I can't help it—I lift up the blanket, letting her in.

She nuzzles and snuggles her way against my chest, curling up again, almost like a cat, wriggling and shifting until she's nestled into my armpit. Her breathing relaxes and slows. She's warm and one ear is soft at my side. It's not a wife, not even a girl-friend, but—hey—it's a warm body. I roll toward her, tucking her into my side, and soon I'm sleeping just as deeply as she is.

She doesn't wake again until almost ten. We're both happy about that. I've got two more days off before I go back to my rotation at work. Two days to figure out what to do with her at night. Two days to make sure she's potty trained. Two more days to get her eating and pooping regularly.

I don't succeed. It doesn't take even a full day to figure out that something's wrong. She's not eating much; she hasn't pooped yet.

I make another round of bacon. The eyes pop open again; she sniffs; she licks. But that's all. I've got tonight off and tomorrow, but after that, I have a series of twelve-hour shifts to navigate—another problem that I'm not ready for.

I had planned to get Maverick patched up, then take her to the humane society. But under the circumstances, with my next shift looming, I decide that the smartest option is to take her there now. They can figure out what's wrong, fork out the money to fix it. I can get back to work and life. That's just logical.

I load Maverick into her cardboard carrier and wind my way to the humane society. She looks out the window through her cone, like this is the best day she's had in her entire life. I swear she's smiling.

We pull into the parking lot and I peer down into her cardboard carrier. She gazes up, soft ears framing her face, mismatched eyes wide and trusting. I shove off the look, close the box, open the car and feel the blast of heat. A hot breeze rustles and I hear her whimper from the box, remember her crying the first night, then remember the little head nuzzled against my side in bed.

She's using her good paw to try to work open the flaps of the box, and I think of the bandaged leg. We're not at a no-kill shelter. As far as I know, we don't have one in town, maybe even in the state. Which means that if her leg is too much…

I put the carrier back in the car, walk to the driver's side, and start the engine.

Maverick looks at me again, like she's asking where we're going now.

I sigh. "Back to the vet's office, you little gold digger." I stare out my window while Maverick looks cheerfully out of hers. I can't afford another thousand dollars. I couldn't afford it the first time, but I really can't now. So if it's going to come to that, I'm going to have to bring her back to the shelter. I have to. Right?

CHAPTER 5

"I need you to help me," I tell the assistant, Rebecca. I don't have to glance at her nametag to remember.

"What's going on?" she says, glancing at the box. Her eyes show real, solid concern. Maverick lets out a yap to show I haven't killed her, and I appreciate that.

"She's not eating; she's barely drinking. She hasn't pooped. But I really don't have another thousand dollars."

"She's not fixed either," Rebecca says, like she's trying to torture rather than help me. "You probably ought to get that taken care of too. Were you planning on breeding her?"

"Look," I say, setting the carrier down. "I actually haven't had her for that long. Honestly—" I suck in a deep breath because I know this isn't the story I told. "—I just found her the other day. She was at the scene of an accident that I was on, and I couldn't get her out of my head later. So I went back and found her. She was hurt. I wanted to help." There. The truth. Done. "But I wasn't really in the market for a dog, and I'm not quite prepared—financially or otherwise."

"You hit her?" she asks, those blue eyes so much harsher than the painted pink lips.

It's a question that confuses me. "Hit her? No, why would I?"

"I mean with your car," she clarifies. "You hit her with your car and you feel guilty. I mean, it's honestly better than a lot of people might have done —" The smile that doesn't hit the eyes the same way. "—and I'm not saying you're responsible to take care of an animal you hit, but…"

"I didn't hit her with my car," I reply.

"You said it was an accident. Did the other person hit her?"

"It wasn't my accident," I say.

Just then the doctor pops out. "Mr. Patterson," she says warmly. "What brings you back so soon?"

"She's not eating right," I say, turning fully from Rebecca, the nosy assistant. Maverick whines pitifully and right on cue.

"Bring her on back," the doctor says and I do, Rebecca following—her face open, her eyes dark.

"Probably just a little infection," Dr. Reynolds replies. "We'll get her set up with some antibiotics—more than the ointment I gave you—and she should be doing better in a couple of days." The vet unwraps the dressing, applies an ointment, rewraps Mavvy's foot, and gives me a small tube of pills.

"He can't afford it," Rebecca says, looking down at the clipboard she's carrying.

I clear my throat. "I wasn't planning on a dog," I say. "I was on a call. I'm a paramedic, and this dog was there, kind of hiding off the road at the scene. I couldn't get her out of my mind."

Rebecca's head pops up for a moment before glancing back down at the clipboard.

The vet hums sympathetically. "You probably could have taken her to the shelter," she says.

"I almost did this morning, but I don't know if they'll keep her with her leg. I thought she might wind up euthanized, and I…"

The doctor waves a hand. "Here," she says, nodding to Rebecca. "We have some meds we generally donate to the humane society. You can have some of those. But a dog's not a small commitment. After she's better, she'll need to be walked and you'll need to figure out what to do with her when you're at work. Long shifts and young dogs don't always play well together. Do you have a neighbor child or something you could pay to help out?"

"Maybe," I reply, racking my brain for neighborhood children. I can only think of old people.

And then, like she knows I have no one to help out, Rebecca adds, "Or you could rehabilitate her and then take her to the shelter. A sweet girl like that will be gone in days."

The words bring a little pang, but I nod like that's a great idea.

"Or you could keep her," the doctor says. "But you'll need a crate for nights, someone to let her out when you work long days."

"I usually work nights," I say quickly.

"That could be good," she says. "Maverick will be sleeping anyway."

I think of her crying and don't feel certain about that at all.

The vet must mistake my look because she adds with a smile, one that meets her eyes, "Or you could do the shelter. It's all up to you. It was kind of you to do what you did. Anything after that is gravy."

Is it, I wonder. When I look down at Maverick who has rested her head on her good paw, I'm not so sure.

CHAPTER 6

"I'd date him myself if I was single," Dr. Reynolds says as I clean the table.

"Hmmm?" I say, like I don't know what she's talking about.

"That guy. He's cute. He rescued a dog. He paid a bunch of money for that dog."

"He lied about finding the dog," I continue. "And now he's apparently flat broke."

"Not uncommon to be flat broke when you just unexpectedly forked out a thousand bucks," she says with an innocent look at her computer screen.

Which is exactly why it seems like the worst idea ever—no money on either side of the fence, mine or his. Who would even pay for dinner? For a second I see us both sitting at a table in a restaurant—him in a tight blue shirt like he was wearing today. I shake it off. Try to replace it with the image of the bill coming. Instead, I just see his face—those dark eyes, his chin scruffy like he hadn't shaved in a couple of days, a nice sort of scruff—sexy firefighter scruff. He's not a firefighter, I remind myself, making the mental correction. Just a guy driving an ambulance.

"And that butt," Dr. Reynolds is saying.

"I didn't look," I reply. It's mostly true. "You shouldn't have either. What would Dan think?"

"He'd think I've still got the eye for a good rump," she replied.

"And the lying part," I say. "Bet Dan didn't start your life together with a bizarre lie."

"Yeah, well, Dan didn't rescue a puppy after potentially saving a life either, so…"

"I don't need someone to date," I grumble.

"You don't," she replies, her feminist side finally taking hold. "Did you decide on a night class?"

I look away from her as I stretch out a fresh bit of paper for the table.

"The last day to sign up for classes is next week," she says.

How she even knows that when my own mother doesn't is beyond me.

"I can't decide. It all feels so important."

"It's not," she says, and I give her a sharp glance. "Not the decision part anyway. Right now you just need to jump on the train, get your feet wet."

"You're mixing metaphors," I say.

"Then take an English class," she replies with a wink. I smile back, but Reynolds has learned what that means. "What have you got it narrowed down to?"

"Something science-y," I reply. It's half true. Those are the classes I'm most interested in, though I'd hardly say I've *narrowed* anything down.

"Science is solid."

I don't answer.

"Look, if it's a money thing, I've been thinking about starting a scholarship for my employees. Maybe you could apply."

"I'd be the only one to apply."

"Then I guess it would work out."

"I can't take your money," I say.

"You wouldn't be taking it."

"And what science would I even take? Chemistry seems too hard."

She frowns. "For you?"

Yes, for me, I want to say like a teenager rolling her eyes at her mother. Instead, I paste on another smile.

But Reynolds isn't going for it. She's looking at Maverick's paperwork.

I'm trying to forget that I actually know the guy's name. Lance, like a weapon for a knight.

"It's not broken," she's murmuring. "I don't know why it got infected so quickly."

"Likely something from the accident got into her skin—one of the deeper layers—and was there too long before we got to her with antiseptic. After all, she was there for a while before she got help."

When Reynolds smiles, I can see I've been tricked. She knew what I was going to say before I said it, but she wanted to hear the words from my show-off lips.

"You could always do zoology," she says, clucking her tongue.

"Don't tell my sister. That's what her plan for me is."

"Mmmm," Reynolds says, putting the paperwork down. "So no zoology. But you know, maybe a little anatomy class might be fun for you," she adds.

I cock my head to the side, picturing the animals that come in. I am fascinated with the way they're put together. And humans…that could be even more interesting. "I mean, maybe."

"Hop on the train," she says. "Get your feet wet."

"Yup. Still a mixed metaphor."

"Take an American literature class."

"I think I'd rather learn about bones."

"Then do it," she says.

There is still the issue of money. I have a little tucked away, but feel nervous spending it when I have no clear career path. And I swear if Reynolds really does do that scholarship thing, I won't apply. I can't just take her money, even if she is practically like a mother to me, even if she does understand the things I want better than my own family—like how she knows this clinic isn't quite the place for me, and that I don't have to be an extension of my sister.

CHAPTER 7

LANCE

The first time Maverick sees a car, she runs after it—or kind of limps after it—trying to bite at the tires. I call to her, trotting after, trying and failing to maintain some modicum of dignity. When the car rounds the corner and speeds up, she finally loses it, and sits on her haunches in a dead pant in the middle of the road.

This is how our first day of training is going. I'm beginning to see how she got mixed up in the car accident.

At least her leg is doing better. Just twenty-four hours later and she's like a new woman. Plus, she seems to be at least partially potty trained. She hasn't pooped on the floor yet, though she did do a little tinkle near the door earlier this morning when I wasn't paying attention to her needs. Also, I'm now officially the kind of guy who says 'tinkle.' Manly.

Speaking of manliness, I scoop her up in my arms and head back home. "We're gonna have to get you a leash, little one."

She gazes at me with her good eye, and I can't help myself, I lean down and put my forehead to hers.

"I've got one more night off work," I tell her when I open the door and let us in. "We'll use tomorrow to get some shopping done. A leash, maybe some toys. And a crate." I give her my best stern look. She gives me her best clueless one. With that foggy eye, she's a natural.

"And tonight we're going to Grandma's house. You'll like that, won't you?"

She wags her tail, like she is absolutely thrilled at the idea of Grandma's house. Good. That makes two of us.

For a brief moment, I toy with the idea of asking my mom to watch her on the nights I'm gone. But even though I know Mom will adore Mavvy, I also know she's not quite ready for that kind of task. Not yet.

I visit my mom several times a week, usually just for a couple hours. It's easier for her that way. She can putter around the kitchen, while I help her make dinner or we can sit in front of the TV and watch reruns of *MacGyver*. She's a huge fan of *MacGyver*. Today I tell her I'm bringing a surprise.

When Maverick pops out of the cardboard carrier (maybe next paycheck I'll replace it with a real one), Mom literally claps with delight, one hand lagging slightly behind the other one so that her clap is lopsided and looks strangely delayed. "I admit I hoped you were bringing me a girl to meet, but I guess this is a good consolation prize." She slurs the words, one half of her mouth not moving up to meet the other quite right, but with the physical therapy, she's making great progress.

"She *is* a girl," I reply.

"And a darling one."

"What more do I need?" I ask.

"Promise me you won't wait till you're old."

Mom blames the trajectory of her life on the fact that she was busy with her career and didn't fall in love the first time until she was nearly forty. I came along about ten months later, much to the delight of my mother, who'd been told she'd never be able to have a baby. And the horror of my father, who'd also been told she'd never be able to have a baby. So I was what some might call an accident. My father definitely did; he left a month after my birth.

Mom hands me a bunch of carrots to chop while Maverick sniffs around her apartment. Using her cane, Mom hobbles her way to the butter, tossing a pat into the pan. I peel and Maverick makes her way into the kitchen, sniffing.

"I told you you'd like it at Grandma's."

"See now," my mom says. "I like the sound of that. *Grandma.* Just don't you stop with this dog."

She stoops low to pet Mavvy's super soft ears and I watch, making sure Mom won't lose her balance and tip over.

"I think we'd better start with the girlfriend before the grandbaby, don't you?" I ask my mom, chopping the carrots into rounds.

"I absolutely think that," Mom says. "It's what I've been trying to say."

I give the carrots a final whack and toss them into the pan with the butter. My mother swirls it around with her good hand, adding a few dashes of salt with her bad one.

"Your mobility is coming back," I say.

"Bit by bit," she replies. "I can now sprinkle salt. Somebody give this old lady an award."

"You're not old," I reply.

"If I wasn't before, I surely am now," she says.

I toss the white fish into the pan and start to chop celery.

"Heard from your dad lately?" she asks.

"Same old same old," I reply. Maverick puts her good front paw on the cupboard door, trying to get closer to the smell of the meat.

Mom sighs.

"Just the checks he still sends *you* to give to *me*," I say. Like I'm still a kid.

"Sometimes he includes a note," she replies.

"Sometimes he includes a brochure for a good law school," I correct.

After he left, I still saw my dad, at least for a few years. He'd come pick me up and take me to a basketball game every time the Kentucky Wildcats played. His alma mater. I guess he figured that was the one true duty of a dad.

We'd stop for hamburgers on the way back to Mom's, and the truth is that I was happy enough with that. At least at that age. But when he got remarried, even the basketball games stopped. I was eight or nine at that point. He shifted to just sending Christmas and birthday presents, maybe with a phone call. Apparently this new match he'd found was his true soul mate, one who didn't feel the need to bother with something as pesky as children, one who would travel all over the world and buy nice furniture and drink fine wines, one he could take to basketball games instead of me. If he still went.

Personally, I'm glad my mom didn't find him till she was forty. By then, she had a career and when he flew away from the nest (had there ever really been a nest), she had a good job, and we had a nice life all our own.

"Watch this, Lance," she says, pouring the cream in a shaky stream into the pot.

I clap.

She bows.

Maverick barks, and we both laugh.

With her good hand, she whisks it all together. "I'll have you break up the fish in a few minutes," she says. "But first taste the broth."

The spoon she holds out for me trembles in her hand, most of it sloshing onto the counter before I can get it into my mouth.

We're working on a seafood bisque, one of her favorites, and something she can't make since the stroke. Not without my help to chop up the fish and vegetables.

"Little more salt," I say, and she pinches the salt from the dish she keeps by the stove. Every day I thank God that He didn't take her mind when the stroke stole her body. She stirs the pot. "Now a little simmer," she murmurs and I help her walk to her favorite chair.

"Laurie coming today?" I ask. She's Mom's home health nurse and comes every day to make sure she's feeling good and 'still alive' (Mom's phrasing, not mine).

"No, I told her you were bringing a girl."

"Which I *did*," I point out again.

My mom sits up a little straighter, though the left shoulder still doesn't move. "Where is she?"

"Uh-oh," I mutter. Maverick is no longer in the kitchen with the yummy food smells, nor is she with us in the living room.

We find her in Mom's bedroom, slurping up the last little bit of Mom's favorite gold necklace—the one I gave her for Christmas last year with a tiny angel dangling from the chain.

I press my fists into my temples. "Bad, bad girl," I say, advancing on her. She shrinks back, like she's fully expecting to be smacked, and I stop and turn back to my mom. "That's another trip to the vet, I guess—to get that thing out. I'm sorry, Mom. I'll replace it for you."

She laughs. "You won't need to replace it. Or go to the vet. She'll poop it out soon enough. You're just going to have to check for it."

"Are you serious?"

"I thought you were a paramedic. Don't tell me you don't deal with poop all the time."

"It's not the part of my job I enjoy dealing with."

"You don't have to dig for it," she says. "I don't need it anyway. Look—" She wobbles her way down to the carpet. "She left the angel. That was my favorite part anyway."

The tiny pendant sparkles from the floor. Mom tries to get it, but her fingers aren't quite nimble enough. Maverick turns a greedy eye toward it, like a dragon ready to add to her hoard.

"Nope," I say to Mavvy, swooping down and rescuing the angel. I help Mom up off the floor, then put the pendant in her jewelry box.

"Usually Laurie helps me put it on," she says. "So I hadn't put it away."

"It's definitely not your fault this happened," I answer. "I'll find the necklace for you. Or get you a new one."

"You will want to be sure it passes," she says. "At least look for it in her stools. You don't have to dig necessarily."

I groan.

"Remember how you liked to suck on pennies," she reminds me. "You accidentally swallowed a few in your day too. Checking poop is something all parents have to do—and I guess dog parents too— dig around in someone else's feces for a little piece of metal."

"No wonder Dad left me." The words slip out before I can stop them.

"He didn't leave you," she says, patting my cheek. "He left me."

"Because you had me," I reply.

"That was just the way the timing worked out. He was done long before you came along."

"He left both of us," I reply, leaning down and kissing her head. She's shrunk at least four inches since the stroke, all of her muscle tone and her skeleton suffering.

"The soup!" she says, wobbling her way back to the kitchen. I take her elbow, just for good measure. Before she hired Laurie, she kept trying to do every- thing herself and had a couple good falls. Fortu- nately a life of working and working out had strengthened her bones sufficiently that she hasn't broken anything yet. But I don't want today to be the day.

"Too bad Laurie's married," she's saying. "You guys would be perfect for each other, fussing over me, like I'm a toddler who can barely walk."

"Too bad Laurie's twice my age and has teenage kids."

"Come on, Maverick," she says, and I'll be darned if that dog doesn't get up and trot after us.

My mom has a gift, or maybe Maverick just remembered the soup.

Which tastes amazing when we finally sit down to eat it.

"See," Mom says, smacking her lips, while holding up the napkin so I can't see the bit I know is dribbling out of the bad side of her mouth. "That stroke didn't take everything from me, not even close. I've still got it."

"You've still got it," I say, smiling though underneath I'm angry about how much the stroke did take. Her job as an engineer, her yoga and pilates classes, her long morning runs. "After dinner, we should take Maverick for a walk."

She glances out the window, making sure the sun

is still bright and high. "I'd like that," she says. "I'd like it a lot."

"You won't even need your walker," I say. "I'll hold your elbow."

"*And* carry the dog?" she asks.

Maverick is sitting on my feet like she's never chased a car in her life. My mom scoops a little bisque with a fat piece of fish into another bowl, only sloshing just the smallest bit, and sets in on the floor by the dog.

Maverick lifts her head, sniffs, and then wobbles her way over to the bowl.

"With that goofy eye, she looks like me," Mom says, laughing.

"Mom!" I say.

"Well, she does," she replies. "No shame in that, little Mavvy. She eats about as neatly too."

Maverick is sloshing soup onto the floor with reckless, happy abandon.

"She knows good food when she sees it," Mom says with more than a little self-satisfaction.

"She did just eat a necklace," I say, teasing her.

"Like I said," Mom replies. "Excellent taste, in all areas."

*I*nstead of carrying her, I tie Maverick up with a bit of rope Mom has in her garage. It looks as white trash as anything you've ever seen, but it does the trick. "We're going to the store tomorrow," I say, holding Mom's elbow.

"I like that you're a boy who makes do," Mom says. And I don't even correct her to tell her I'm not a boy.

Maverick poops on the walk. Mom glances sideways at me. "It's probably too soon," she says.

Even so, when I lean down and scoop it up with the plastic bag, I hold it up to the sun, looking for glints of metal.

"Welcome to parenthood," Mom says, taking my arm again. "Now to find you a girl to go with it."

I open my mouth to answer that Maverick is a girl, but Mom intercepts before I can get the words out. "A *human* girl."

Both of us laugh and the summer sun goes a little golden, stretching its arms across the horizon, pinking at the edges.

"A perfect sunset," Mom says. "Amazing what comes to us every day, even in this imperfect world."

I pull her a little closer, feeling her warmth as we walk the short block home.

CHAPTER 8

BECCA

In the end, I can't decide on ONE class. In the end, I pick two.

Anatomy and Biology. They seem like a good pairing.

And even though I didn't fill out a single word on a single scholarship application, I've got a $500 bonus on my paycheck this week. There's no easy way to return it. And it's enough for a class at the community college. I've got my own $500 saved up for the other.

Summer semester starts soon—next week to be exact. One is Monday night; the other Wednesday. Both three-hour classes.

I buy each of the textbooks online, and the anatomy one gives me a free epacket. Sweet. I open it and start reading the first unit. Skin. I flip forward to the bones, thinking about the injured animals my sister used to drag home, thinking of the hundreds I've seen in Reynolds' clinic since then. Thinking of the amazing things modern medicine can do, even for animals, if you just have enough information.

I read through dinner, until my head starts bobbing and I realize it's nearly ten o'clock. Anatomy for the win, I think, clicking away from the ebook.

S ally Mae texts me as my head hits the pillow. Does that woman never sleep (answer: possibly not)? "You interested in an editing job? Just one. Allen is fantastically busy with work right now, and it would lighten his load."

Allen is her husband, and her normal editing guy. But he's working toward a promotion. And, uh, I'm not.

It's late. I could ignore the text, but then it will just bug me all night.

"How much?" I reply. I mean, how much editing does she have; how long will it take. But she replies with the rate she'll pay.

"Fifty bucks an hour."

Not bad. It's more than triple what I make at Reynolds' office. But I still don't want to.

"You know editing isn't really my thing."

"You're good at it," she replies.

She's not wrong.

"It's just one job," she adds. "To help Allen out."

Sure, sure, for Allen and all. Like I'd be more inclined to help my brother-in-law over my sister.

"Send it over and I'll have a look at it," I text. "Got to get some sleep tonight."

"'Kay. We'll talk more Sunday.

Yippee. It's not that I hate editing. It's not that I never want to work for an awesome Girl Boss. It's just that it's a whole other messy beast when Girl Boss is your big sister—aka, when she's been your Girl Boss from the womb. What I need is something she's not at all interested in, something that will allow me to be her sister, not another assistant.

CHAPTER 9

LANCE

My last morning off. It's time to figure some stuff out. Like what to do with Mavvy while I'm gone. And how to keep her occupied when I'm not. We've got no toys, no treats, and I can't even take her to the park because I don't have a leash.

She looks at me like she read my mind and she's dying to go to the park. "Okay, okay," I say. "But first we've got to go to the store."

I've seen people walking their dogs into those stores. It seems like a fun outing. (Am I now taking my animal on dates? My mom is going to flip.) And maybe if I can tucker her out enough during the day, she'll just fall asleep at night. But I still don't have a leash, and I left the rope at Mom's house.

I decide I'll bring her with me in her cardboard crate, then get a leash, hook her up, leaving the price tag on, and pay for it as I go through the line. It's not my easiest plan ever, mostly because as Maverick has recovered, she is completely uninterested in being contained in that carrier. I load her up anyway, and she gnaws at the cardboard edges. She'll have a hole in it by the time we go home if I don't hurry. So I guess I should buy another carrier too. One that can't be gnawed apart in ten minutes. With a real carrier, we could go places together. Like people with dogs do—well, like old ladies with dogs do, anyway.

As I walk into the store, I get more than a few odd looks. People probably think I've got a lizard or snake or something and not a dog. At least that's what I hope they think when I see the sideways glances.

I rush to the leash aisle as quickly as possible, which isn't very quickly considering I have no idea where it is. There's a picture of a dog on one of the walls and I hurry that direction. Sure enough, it's the dog zone, but it's huge. I wander each aisle like a lost soul, with a random animal in a cardboard box, when I stumble onto the leashes. "Thank goodness," I grumble. I'm working the leash and matching collar out of the cardboard casing when an employee wanders over and I realize how this must look. She stares at me. I clear my throat, setting Maverick, box and all, on the floor. "Hey," I say. "I was going to buy this leash, but I was wondering if I could use it in the store with her first." I clear my throat again.

The teenager gives me one of those shrug-whatever looks that they're good at, then watches me as I struggle with the plastic pieces meant to hold it on. I can't get them off, so I end up ripping off the cardboard and leaving the plastic—I'll cut it off at home. "You'll need the sku from the cardboard," the teenager says.

I nod, picking it up, along with my cardboard box. "Um, do you have any of these carriers? Except not cardboard," I say, sounding like I've never actually left my house or talked to another human in my entire life.

"Um, aisle eight, I think," the teenager says. "And you'll probably need a cart."

She doesn't offer to get me one.

From down the aisle, I hear a giggle. A long, gorgeous brunette with a white Maltese on a leash that she actually owns is smiling in my direction. "First time?" she asks.

"How did you know?" I grumble, dragging my

assortment of cardboard items along with me.

"Here," she says. "Leave those with me and go grab a cart. Also, the carriers are probably just around the corner, not in aisle eight. Teens these days, right?"

She can't be more than twenty-five, which makes her comment even more funny. Against the nearly black hair, her eyes are a mesmerizing brown. I fall into them for a minute before nodding and dragging Maverick, who feels the need to smell every item in the store, toward the carts.

When I return with the cart, the woman is on her phone texting.

"Thanks," I sigh, heaving the boxes in, and then setting Maverick down on the floor.

The woman glances up from her phone. "Any time," she responds. "I'm one of the vets here, so if you ever need any help, just let me know. Victoria." She holds out a delicate hand for me to shake.

I take it. It's warm, soft, and perfectly manicured. "Lance," I reply. Then, feeling a little like Maverick, I tip my head to the side in a question. "You're a vet here?" I ask, not sure which part I'm more puzzled about—the fact that she's old enough to be an actual veterinarian, or the fact that veterinarians work in the pet store.

"Yeah, we have a partnership with PetStop."

"Cool," I say, only because the thousand questions I have about Maverick's leg and eye and everything else have fled from my mind.

"Of course, looks like you've already got somebody good, so don't feel like I'm trying to drag you away from them. That's not my style."

"No, sure," I say, then—because my mouth is running faster than my brain— "Hey, do you want to get coffee after this? There's a shop down the way."

She smiles, but there's something in it now, little wrinkles at the edges of her eyes. "I can't," she replies. "Not today."

"Could I get your number then?" I ask, not yet worried that my brain still hasn't caught up with my mouth.

"Also not today," she says with that laugh. "I've got a boyfriend."

"Oh, sorry." It's then that my brain catches up, and my face gets hot.

"Nothing to be sorry about. I'll see you around," she says, and the white Maltese follows along her side like it doesn't even need that leash.

She's out of sight by the time I snap out of it. Maverick helps me by stumbling into my leg as she noses the things on the bottom shelf. I tug her back slightly, finally looking at the array of choices in front of me. All the carriers, supplies, everything. I ask Maverick if she has an opinion, but she's too busy sniffing a dead bug she's found on the floor.

I've just chucked the cheapest black carrier I can find into the cart when I see a familiar face—well, familiar back of the head. Red curls tumbling almost to her waist. I've already struck out once today, but she turns before I can scoot out of the aisle, and then I've got to say something.

"Hey," I begin.

Maybe I didn't need to say anything at all because it takes her a second to recognize me—a second plus a quick glance at Maverick, whom she does recognize. "Oh, hi…"

"Lance," I fill in for her.

"Right. It's tricky seeing people out of context."

Yeah, sure, except that I am in a pet store with the very pet that she just treated. Buying a carrier like she suggested. It's not that far out of context. "What do you think?" I hold the carrier up.

She nods without a lot of commitment. "Looks great. You planning to take her to a lot of vets or something?"

The comment catches me slightly off guard. "I mean, no. Just for when we drive."

She gives me a funny look. "Most people just let the dogs ride in their passenger seat next to them."

I shrug, feeling a little like an idiot. "Yeah, well, with my job—I guess I just wanted a way to belt her in."

Rebecca nods again, but more thoughtfully this time. "Um, about that. I'm really sorry for what I said —about the accident."

"About me hitting this dog with my car and then bringing her in to your office out of guilt?"

"It's not my office," she says. "And, yes—about that."

"Does that happen a lot—people accidentally hit animals and bring them in?"

"It happens occasionally. Although usually the family just finds the poor animal after it's been hit by someone who left, and then they bring them in. If the animal is still alive. And, honestly, sometimes if they're not. People hope for miracles."

"Now that part sounds a LOT like my job," I say.

She smiles again and for the first time I notice her teeth, straighter and whiter than any I've seen in real life. My brain is starting to lag again and I almost comment on them, but stop myself.

"Anyway," she continues, looking down at her cart, which contains several dozen dog chews. "It wasn't cool of me to assume you'd hit her. And definitely not cool to accuse you of hitting her. It's just that—" She stops without finishing.

"You could tell I was lying."

The smile brightens even more when I say it, though she quickly tucks the full smile away. "That happens sometimes too," she says.

"Maybe we actually work the same job," I say with a wink.

Maverick is starting to whine. Rebecca lifts an eyebrow and nods toward the front door. "You better take her out. She's going to pee on the floor if you don't."

Are. You. Even. Kidding. Me. I thought dogs were supposed to help you pick up women, not interrupt every potential conversation you could be having. "Okay," I say. "Um, do you mind watching the cart?"

"Yeah, sure," she says.

I turn toward the door and Maverick rushes toward it, tugging a little desperately at the leash. We hurry through the automatic doors and I hear the alarm going off just as I hear the whiz of Maverick peeing.

A balding man is glaring at me, heading my direction, as a little yellow river trickles down the sidewalk in front of the store.

"You need to pay for that leash," he says just before glancing down.

I can tell that his brain is struggling to catch up too.

"I'm sorry, sir. I was shopping and she had to go, so I rushed out."

He sighs. "We'll have to hose that off."

"I'm really sorry," I say.

"Please return to the store, pay for your items, and leave."

At that moment, the brown-eyed veterinarian, Victoria, walks through the exit past us. "Is there a problem, Ted?"

"No, just—" He waves around angrily at the mess and at me.

"A new customer with a new dog," she says pointedly.

He smiles at her. I mean, who wouldn't. It's a real smile too, and I realize that every guy who works here is probably disappointed that she's got a boyfriend. If, in fact, she really does. Maybe it's just something she says to get people off her back.

"You should help him if he needs anything more," she says, before beeping her car, so it unlocks. And not just any car—a red Mercedes. Sure enough, it's in a spot reserved for the vet.

Her little Maltese trots over to it, then stands at attention beside the door, like a tiny soldier, but Victoria doesn't walk to the car yet. She waits for the employee to do what she said.

"Sure," he says, heading back inside, presumably to look for a hose to hook up, just as Rebecca makes her way to the exit doors, lugging our carts.

She leaves the carts just inside the doors so the buzzer doesn't go off again. "Thought you got lost," she says to me before realizing who I'm talking to. "Oh, hi, Dr. Voyle." She gives a polite nod.

Hearing Rebecca refer to the other woman who looks younger than she is as 'doctor' just feels so weird on so many levels for me.

"Hey Rebecca. A friend of yours?" She nods to me.

"He brought his new dog in for treatment," she replies. When she says it, her voice sounds just a little cold.

"Then you're in good hands," Victoria replies.

Dr. Victoria Voyle. Could there be a sexier, more powerful name?

She clicks another button and the driver's side of her car opens. Her dog hops into the back seat without so much as a command and Victoria walks to her car.

It's then that I realize I'm just standing there, gaping. I turn back to Rebecca, to my own cart.

"Wow, she's got a nice car," I say, trying to make up for the staring.

"She definitely has a nice car," Rebecca replies and that chill creeps into her voice again.

The sweet Mercedes zooms away and it's then that a little voice in the back of my mind (I think the voice is attached to my actual brain, which is struggling today) tells me I need to get away from the front of the store before grumpy Ted returns with a hose.

It's then that Rebecca notices the pee and puts everything together. She kind of snort-laughs, and I kind of laugh back. Maverick looks up at both of us like we've lost our minds before sniffing her own pee daintily.

"Here," Rebecca says, nodding toward the cart just inside the doors. "Put her in here and I'll help you get what you need so you can leave. You're going to have to time it so that they can clean this up before you go."

I groan. She's right. I do not want to pass anyone while they're cleaning up the mess my own dog made. "Thanks, Rebecca."

"Call me Becca," she replies. "Now, what else do

you need?" She's walking back into the store with purpose as I steer the cart after her.

"Maybe some of those poop bags," she says. "Of course you could just recycle the plastic bags from the grocery store. A toy or two for sure. Bed maybe?"

"I was actually just going to get a carrier and the leash," I say, trailing after her. But just then we hit the aisle of toys, and Maverick's little puppy eyes bug out of her head like we've arrived at Disneyland. She eyes several of the balls like she's waiting for them to hop off the shelves and into her mouth.

"Here," Becca says. "My sister loves these things for her dogs." She hands me a couple of tennis balls stuck in a holder. "You use it to throw the ball. That way you don't get your hands all slobbery."

I toss one in the cart. I get all the bodily fluids I need at work.

"You'll want extra balls too. They go through them fast. Maybe a stuffy toy with a squeaker in it."

She squeaks the squeaker and Maverick wags her tail like she's on dog crack. I just pray that she won't get so excited she pees in the cart too. I'm not sure I could handle it today.

"And these bones help their teeth stay clean and strong." Becca stuffs some bones and a few things labeled 'pig ears' into my arms.

"They're not actually pig ears, right?" I say.

She glances at them like she's never thought to wonder before. "Probably not. Probably more like really really hard jerky. So maybe pig something. And, I mean, they could be the ears."

A pragmatist. I like that.

When I think we're finished, she leans over and gently takes Maverick's paw in her hand, moving the leg just a bit. "Hmmm," she says. "It'd be nice if there was something to keep that from getting too stiff."

She pushes it back and forth, watching Maverick's face to be sure she doesn't take it too far and hurt her. "You know, four in five people need rehab after things like this. There's nothing like that for dogs. Not that I know of anyway."

"Well, maybe you should be the first," I say with a smile.

"Truth be told, I'm more interested in humans. Dogs always seem to figure it out. We don't."

"Why not?" I wonder out loud.

She shrugs. "Who knows? Maybe we really don't need physical therapy and it's just something we created to make money."

"Or maybe we do," I say. "And someone figured out that they could help people improve their quality of life so they didn't have to spend the next fifty years of it limping around and having constant pain after an accident."

Her eyes open up. It feels just like when it's been rainy for days and you're not sure you'll ever see the sun again and then one morning you wake up and the whole room is light and you walk outside and your eyes soak in the blue sky and yellow sun and green, green plants. That's how it feels.

"You ever been hurt?" she asks. "At your job?"

"Not like that," I say, though I think of my mother, one half of her face and body hanging low when I know her heart is working so hard to raise them up.

"Me either," she says like it's a bad thing, a failing of some sort. "Better get you to the register before you go broke."

"I *was* just going to get a leash and a carrier," I point out.

"You'll thank me when she doesn't eat your entire couch."

Loaded up with every conceivable thing I could possibly need, we make our way to the checkout.

Becca does a little calculation in her head. "Here," she says. "I've got a coupon for twenty percent off."

"No, it's okay," I respond, holding up a hand and remembering how I complained to Dr. Reynolds about how I couldn't afford another thousand dollars. "I've got it," I say.

"Don't be silly," she replies. "You've got all that stuff, and I've got—" She looks down into her own cart like she can't remember. "—I've got the dog chews that my sister asked me to pick up."

"She has a lot of animals, huh?" I ask as the checker rings up my items.

"You have no idea," Becca replies.

"Must run in the family," I say, handing over the coupon and then my credit card.

"Yeah," she replies, the lips closing over the teeth.

"You do, um, like animals, right?" I push my cart forward so she can check out.

"Of course I like animals," she says. "I'm not a psychopath."

"But you don't have any," I press just slightly as she checks out her items. I realize I'm waiting for her.

"How do you know?" We walk to the parking lot together, both of us sidestepping the freshly hosed-off section of the sidewalk.

I nod at the bag in her hand. "Any pet owner wouldn't have come just to do one small errand for her sister."

"That's true," she says. "I guess my sister has

enough animals for us both." She reaches down to pet Maverick on the head. "And a YouTube channel based around animals and a successful career based around animals. You should check it out."

"Her career?" I ask.

"No," she says with a laugh—one that shows her teeth. "Her YouTube channel. Full of inspiring stories."

Then she stops, just like that, right in the middle of the parking lot.

"My car's just here," I say.

She looks at me, a little line creasing her forehead, before she takes in a breath that erases it. "In fact, you might be the perfect fit for her channel—you and Maverick."

"What do you mean?" I ask.

"She does inspiring stories. With animals. You—an EMT."

"Paramedic," I correct.

"Is there a difference?"

"Yeah, EMTs just do basic stuff. I can give meds, and do more complex procedures, like intubations."

The eyebrow tips up. "Anyway, you, a paramedic. You find this dog—wounded from an accident that you were on. You save the dog." She fans out her fingers in a jazz hands sort of way.

"That does sound inspiring," I say. "But I'm not sure I could do that show."

"Why not?" she asks.

"The accident wasn't really a happy ending. I mean, maybe for Maverick, but…"

"Oh shoot," she says. "I'm so sorry. Someone got hurt."

I look at her. "Yeah," I say, not mentioning that one person got really hurt, and that the wife of thirty years died from the accident. It's not the type of thing people like to hear, especially people with inspirational YouTube channels.

"Okay, well, scratch that. Maybe. Of course, Sally Mae could find a way to work it so it was sensitive. She always does."

"Sally Mae," I say, trying to change the topic. "Your sister."

"Yeah," she replies. "Boss Girl extraordinaire."

It's a funny thing to say about your sister, especially a sister with an inspirational animal YouTube channel and the name Sally Mae.

At the door of my car, Becca pauses, just for the briefest moment. I glance at the coffee shop just a few shops down the strip mall. And there goes my brain again, off the rails. "Hey, if you'd like, we could grab a coffee together." I nod to the building.

"Oh, no, that's okay," she says. "I've got to get this stuff to Sally Mae anyway."

I nod. "So, do you think, if I ever have questions about Maverick—could I maybe call you?"

"Not sure I'm the one you'd want to call, but you can always call the office."

Ouch. Two strikes. I don't need to go for a third. "I will," I say, then clamber into my car.

She scuttles toward her own—a little inexpensive Ford Taurus. She sways when she walks, the hair shifting along her back with the rhythm of it.

I look away and start my car. "I thought everyone could use a little late morning coffee," I say, looking at Maverick for some comfort.

Maverick has instantly fallen asleep in the warm sun from her window, but she pops her good eye open when she hears my voice.

"You would have given me your number, right?" I ask. "Like, I don't have fungus growing out of my skin or anything."

She sniffs the new carrier, and I wonder if fungus would really deter her.

I put my hand over the top of her head and she reaches up with her snout and nuzzles it. *Of course I would have given you my number,* the nuzzle says.

"Thanks, girl," I reply.

CHAPTER 10

LANCE

I realize when I get home that I didn't buy a crate for Maverick to sleep in. Maybe that was unconsciously intentional, because I realize that I really hate the idea of it. But I also realize that she's napped the entire way home, and that if I want her tuckered out, I'm going to have to do better than that.

I cut the plastic bits off the leash—the ones I couldn't remove in the store—and then tear open one of the ball toys Becca insisted on. "Alright, Maverick," I say. "You ready for your first official walk?"

She wags her tail, but then walks in a circle, like she's fixing to take another nap. I clip the leash onto her little collar and she looks at it quizzically. Then I open the door, and she's up on her legs, even tugging a bit with the injured leg.

"That's my girl," I say.

And we're off, Maverick dragging me along, peeing and pooping with delight (good thing we bought those poop bags). When we get to the park, I pull out the first tennis ball. Maverick eyes it. And then I throw.

The gimpy leg slows her down a little, though her foggy eye proves to be her biggest handicap. It throws off her aim. She misses the ball sometimes when it's right in front of her, topples to the left when another inch would get it right into her mouth. In general, she stumbles around like a three-legged, drunken man. Which is maybe the cutest thing I've ever seen.

"We could dress you up with a pirate costume for Halloween," I tell her, rolling the ball for the thousandth time. She hop-trots toward it, then skids past it, looking around like I've done a magic trick and the ball has vanished, only to find it a few inches to her left. This doesn't stop her from scooping it up like she's the sharpest tool in the shed and proudly limp-walking it back to me.

We don't leave until dinnertime, and by the time I get back to my townhouse, I have to lift her up because she's practically falling asleep on the sidewalk. "Ha," I murmur in her ear. "My little plot has worked."

I take her into my bedroom and put her next to the bed. She looks up sleepily, waiting for me to lift her, like we've gotten in the habit of doing. "You've got to learn to do it yourself," I say.

She puts her good front paw against the comforter that hangs down, then whines for me to help.

"Just a minute," I say, going into the kitchen and digging out a wooden box. I bring it back, put it next to the bed. "Come on," I say, tapping it.

She steps up onto it, then looks up at the bed, and with the cutest little jump, she's in.

She sits there, waiting for me to climb in too. "Mavvy, I've got to go to work tonight. I look at my pajama pants flung on the floor, grab them along with a t-shirt I haven't washed yet. I lay them on my bed, making a little cushion out of them. "Come on, girl."

Maverick sniffs and, finding the unwashed scent of my clothes too amazing to pass up, she pads onto them, walking her little circle, then plopping down. She's asleep instantly. Good thing, too. Because I'm almost late for work.

When I arrive, I'm surprised to see a white Ford truck instead of Callen's blue Toyota sitting in the parking lot.

"Hey Jordan," I say when I walk in. "Long time, no see."

"Hey kid," Jordan says. He's got the keys for the ambulance, ready to check it out for the start of our shift.

"So?" I begin. "Where's Callen?"

"Didn't you hear?" Jordan asks. "Oh, I guess you took a day off last week. Callen took a leave of absence. Just a couple of weeks. That last call really threw him."

"Shoot," I say, drawing the 'o' out.

"Don't worry. He'll work it out. I told him to take his time and I'd cover for him for a bit."

"That's nice of you," I say.

"Sure is," he adds. "After all, I have to work with you again."

I laugh. Jordan has been here forever. He was the medic that trained me seven years ago. In a field of rough and tumble older guys, he's a big old panda bear. Almost like a grandfather to all of us.

"You think Callen will be alright?" I ask. "He took

it really hard."

"I think he'll be alright," Jordan says. "That first loss is always a tough one, isn't it?"

"Yeah," I mutter. And it is. I remember mine. A diabetic it seems like we should have been able to save. But we didn't. I push the thought away.

"How's Emily?" I mutter.

"Gorgeous as ever."

I smile. They've been married for forty years. "She still come to the station to bring you dinner?"

"Oh, sometimes. When I told her who my partner was she refused."

I glance at him.

He slaps my back. "Just kidding, Lance. She said she's bringing cookies. Those macadamia nut ones you always loved." Jordan drags the syllables out for macadamia, deep Kentucky style.

I salivate at the thought. Emily can cook like nobody in this world.

"You got anybody new in your life?" Jordan says, hanging up his jacket. "You can't survive off of my wife's cooking forever, you know."

"I cook," I say defensively.

"Tastes better when you cook with a pretty girl." He pauses. "Speaking of, how's your little mama doing?"

"She's getting better," I say, happy to change the subject.

"Glad to hear it," he replies.

Before he can say anything else, the tones go off. We look at each other, and the night begins.

Maverick is just getting up and stretching when I get home. I take her out to do her business, and congratulate myself on my absolutely perfect plan.

I feel myself leaning against the door as she takes her time sniffing grass and rocks and finding the perfect spot. It was a busy night. Two fender benders that didn't really need us, but called anyway. An older lady who fell. Some kid who OD'd—that was a rough one, but we got him to the hospital and he'll likely survive. And then a lady who cut her leg with a sharp pair of scissors when she was trying to help her daughter with a school project at the crack of dawn this morning.

My eyes are drooping by the time Maverick comes back, wagging her tail and eyeing the leash and tennis balls I've hung up on the coat rack. "Not now, little girl," I say, stripping off my work clothes and staggering to the bedroom.

She follows, tail still wagging.

I crash into bed, and she hop hops her way up into it. "Ready for another nap already, are you?" I ask, yawning.

She plants a paw again against my hand. I rub her neck, already halfway asleep. She digs into the blanket, makes her cat-like circle, and snuggles into my armpit.

Seven hours later, I wake to find her gone, along with my left boot for work. When I uncover it a few minutes later, it's missing a chunk of leather in the heel. I holler her name. She ignores me. Two more times before she limps in, tail between her legs, unwilling to look at me. It's then that my life as a dog owner really begins.

"Bad dog," I say, and it's the most redundant thing I've probably ever uttered in my life because she clearly already feels bad. Which doesn't mean, I realize, looking into that face and watching her nose twitch at the familiar smell of the apparently delicious leather, that she won't do it again. Addicts, dogs—repeating the same bad behaviors and feeling guilty every time, but still doing it again. I guess that's one thing that makes dogs different than cats, who just live out their sins without the guilt weighing them down. Those boots, or whichever ones I have to buy to replace them—they're going to have to go in a box or closet that I keep shut.

It won't be the only thing either. I go through the house, starting in the hallway. I know lots of people tell these stories about dogs ripping stuff up like it's so cute, because it kind of is when they get into stuff and dump out the trash and look guilty. But also, it's kind of not, and I'm not a rich enough man to replace everything I own within the next month. I look at Maverick. The vet thinks she's between twelve and fourteen months old. Prime mischief time.

I assess my house like it's the first time I'm seeing it, then walk through the hall. No more shoes can hang out there. I'll have to buy one of those benches that opens so I can store them; that or I'll have to keep them in the closet, and keep that shut. As for the living room, all the pillows will need to be put in the closet while I'm asleep. Hopefully she won't chew on the couch legs or anything—that would be obnoxious. The carpet is also a concern. Since she was barely eating at first, it's hard to know how well she's potty trained, although she's been a rock star so far.

I sigh, moving into the kitchen. The trash is the biggest problem. I'll need a can with a lid for sure, and to start keeping the pantry door closed so she can't get into the chips, or anything worse. In my bedroom, well, the laundry should have gotten moved off my floor years ago; I guess now is the time. All shoes out of sight. Belts, hung up. Tissues, no longer on my end table for months on end. Bathroom trash, yikes, up on the back of the toilet, I guess.

When I'm done with my assessment, I'm literally sweating, though Maverick is looking like she's got energy for days and she's tugging at the leash hanging from its hook. "Okay, okay," I say. "A trip to the park." I carry my now full laundry basket to the washing machine and start a load. I've got another shift tonight and need to get this dog tuckered out.

Just then, she starts to whine. "Hang on," I holler from the laundry room. "Just give me a second."

The whining stops.

By the time I make it into the hall, Maverick is sitting in a miserable heap on the floor and there's a little pile of poo beside her. "Oh, girl," I say.

But then I see a little glitter of gold poking out. And I start to laugh.

CHAPTER 11

BECCA

Lance's smile is lopsided.

I dig into my brand new anatomy book, trying to understand why that would happen. Things like trauma or childhood stress could cause it, but it seems the most likely culprit is the teeth—maybe a molar that's missing or different from the other side. It could even have happened because he chewed or sucked too much on one side as a baby.

I stare at the sinewy sketches in my anatomy book, aware that I would never in a million years want to fix that lopsided smile no matter what caused it.

Which doesn't mean I don't want to know why. Why why why? Why would one man be half a head taller than me with long arms, long legs, tight torso and chest, bright brown eyes with a lopsided smile and beautiful front teeth when another would be shorter, stouter, maybe stronger—muscles in tight balls instead of long lines. Eyes blue or green or tan instead of the creamy dark chocolate. And why, why on earth would someone be attracted to one of those men and less so to another?

My anatomy book lies helplessly in front of me, unable to answer that last question. Should I take a psychology class next? And of those two men, why would one save an animal when another would ignore it? Why would anyone lie about any of it at all, and if he did—even for a short time—would that be a red flag for someone?

Head. Back. In. The. Game.

Not questions I need to be asking. Nope. I tip my face back down to the image of the muscles of the shoulder. Rhomboid, trapezius, deltoid, subscapularis, supraspinatus, infraspinatus, teres minor. I

think about how the joints and ligaments affect those muscles, and how they all work together, how one part can throw the whole system off, giving someone unbearable pain or limiting their mobility.

Maybe not quite as interesting as how smiles work, but pretty close. And exactly where my focus should be. So why am I thinking of smiles and men and potential attractions? Why am I worrying about psychology and genetics and other subjects. Why, when I'm supposed to be faithful to my anatomy book, do all those other things keep popping up?

No wonder Mom said I shouldn't waste my time in college until I knew what I wanted, shouldn't waste my time with men till I knew what they were about. Both could be expensive, time consuming, and confusing. Which is how I'm feeling right now.

That guy. Lance Patterson. Manliest name ever. I thought he was just a lying jerk—the kind of guy who hits a dog, brings it to the vet, hoping to cover his sins and then get rid of it. Not the worst kind of man (that sort leaves the dog to die or be found by some neighborhood kid on her way to school). But not the best kind of man either. Not the kind of man who spends his career taking care of emergencies and then rescues a dog on the call and pays for its care out of his—per the internet (yeah, I looked it up) —not too chunky paycheck. Not the kind who shows up at PetStop with a cardboard carrier and a slightly desperate look on his face.

I smile thinking of the face, and again, of that lopsided grin. My mind trips back to my book. Orbicularis oculi and zygomaticus—the muscles of smiling. A look another mind will perceive as attractive.

Strange things, these bodies. Strange and beautiful.

And maybe the strangest thing of all is that someone would turn down a coffee date with that person, even though she really wanted to do it. (Where *is* that psychology class when I need it?)

It seems silly to think that Lance would ask me for coffee again, not with that turn down, but Sally Mae really needed those chews.

Or maybe I'm just nervous about adding one more thing to my life. The last boyfriend I had was in college. I dropped out of college to try to make it work (and also because college definitely wasn't working). We didn't make it work. Then I played for a while, and got burned a few more times that way.

By the time I decided I wanted to get serious about things, Sally Mae was married with a couple of babies, and her YouTube channel was taking off. Which meant that by the time I was ready to get serious about things I was pegged (permanently, it seems) as the irresponsible, happy-go-lucky little sister, fun aunt, job-hopping kid.

I sigh. Maybe I should permanently take that editing job for Sally. It would help her, Allen, me.

Everybody. And at least that way I'd get paid for the million things she asks me to do. Or at least I'd get paid for one of the things she asks me to do.

Not that I even need to get paid for helping her out. After all, she's my sister, and isn't helping the sort of thing that sisters do? It's what I'd do for my friend. And sisters should be friends. Not co-workers. Or is working for her the way we would grow closer?

My alarm goes off.

Time for dinner.

Family dinner. Every Sunday night.

It's unfair to say that I dread it, except that I dread it. I mean, I love my family. They would do anything for me, which also means that they expect anything given in return.

And, hey, if we're talking about giving up an emergency kidney, I'm totally down with that.

But if we're talking about me playing errand girl for the rest of my life, that seems a little harder.

Mom already acts like Sally Mae and I are part of the same corporation, but also not like we're partners. Sally is the CEO, and I'm the girl who buys coffee for everyone.

"What's the story this week?" Mom says eagerly as soon as Sally has settled in to her spot. Allen is bringing the kids later. Sally came straight from the studio where she was recording.

"Not sure yet," Sally says. "I just recorded a few backups, but nothing's quite calling to me."

Those were stories I helped her get—a few couples who got their animals into surgery just in time.

"Well, at least you've got something," Mom says like she doesn't.

"Yeah," Sally replies, also like she doesn't. "Anything new at the office, Becca?"

"I wasn't aware I was in charge of programming," I grumble, pulling the salad plate toward me and dumping a generous serving of ranch over the top.

"It's meant to be served with a vinaigrette," Mom says. "I was going to toss it for everyone when Allen arrived."

Sally clicks her phone off with a sigh. "He's not coming," she says. "Geraldine just barfed in the car."

"Carsick?" Mom asks.

"Most likely," Sally replies.

For a split second, I think about the way the

inner ear senses movement while the eyes see a static view, and the disconnect in the brain sometimes causes motion sickness.

I almost say this, along with a brief discussion of the inner ear, then choke it right back down. Sally is texting like crazy, and a sermon about the inner ear doesn't seem super helpful under the circumstances.

"I probably better go and help out."

Her phone dings again. She reads it, looking as though she's trying to decide if she should tell the truth about it or not.

"What?" Mom asks.

"Allen says I can stay, that it's no big deal. 'Enjoy your lady time.' That's what he wrote."

"Like Dad doesn't count," I say.

"Dad's not coming," Mom says. "You know the fiscal year ends in July."

As far as I can tell, it's time for business if Dad's not in the mood for dinner. He's probably at a burger joint right now instead of getting his salad dressed with vinaigrette. "But you set a place for him," I say.

"I'm saving it," she replies. And that's that.

"So, are you staying?" I ask Sally, not sure what I want the answer to be. Just me and Mom *would* feel lonely.

"I'll stay for a bit. If she keeps puking, I'll head home. If she's just carsick, then Allen will be happy to stay with the kids and watch the game."

Aha. Another reason Dad's business may have invaded. Too bad they both didn't come; they could have watched baseball together, not that the matriarchy in my family would ever approve of something so mundane on family dinner night.

Sally is talking about different ideas for the show —maybe a pony with a broken leg who is now at a petting zoo, bringing joy to disabled children and allowing kids with sensory issues to pet and comb him. It's a good story, but she can't get the interview in time for this week.

"We had a guy come in this week," I say when she comes up for air.

"A *guy*," Sally says.

"Yeah," I say quickly, "but that's not the point. He had a dog."

"You don't say," Sally says. She's joking and for a minute the tension of the last few years eases between us and we're just two sisters teasing each other about boys.

"The dog was hurt."

"No," Sally says in mock shock.

I toss my napkin at her, smiling.

"Anyway, maybe a show about the dog. It hurt its leg and this guy saved it from a car accident."

"Did he hit it?" my sister and mother ask at the same time. It's easy to see that the apple doesn't fall too far from the tree. I think about what genetics might create this, or maybe it's just a matter of nurture. Whether hereditary or learned, it's definitely our family style.

"No," I say, leaving out all the parts about him being a paramedic, and about someone getting hurt. I'm worried Sally would want to do the story anyway and it was clear that Lance thought it'd be a bad idea. "I was just thinking that maybe once the dog is better, you could do a show on animal rehabilitation."

"You're kidding," Sally says.

"Animals are truly amazing," I add. "Think about it. People spend months and years in rehab. These animals just glue back together and then go on with their lives.

"Hmmm," Sally says. "I'll think about it for a future episode, though I still don't have anything solid for this week."

I regret again that Lance doesn't like the idea of a story with him and Maverick in it. It'd be a good angle for Sally.

After all, there's a reason those firefighter-puppy calendars sell so well. Hot guys, cute animals. Muscles and sweetness.

I pause on the thought of Lance without a t-shirt for just a second, then shake out of it.

Probably some HIPAA violation or something if he does the story and talks about his job. I'd hate for him to lose his job over a show with Sally. Still, the thought sits there.

A paramedic and puppy episode. It'd be pretty epic.

But it would require contacting him, talking to him, getting to know him.

That thought sits with me for a few more seconds. I try to shake it off too—after all, I'm going to be so busy—though it doesn't shake as well.

And not just because I know the show would be great.

CHAPTER 12

LANCE

It's been several weeks. Maverick has learned to sit, fetch (goofy eye aside), and roll over (my favorite; it's so cute). She mostly trots happily beside me on our walks now, except when she sees a squirrel, or a particularly luscious bit of garbage.

She's only torn up one other pair of shoes—some soccer slides, which I left out in a moment of weakness. She's walking better, though she still has a slight limp, and I wonder occasionally if there's anything I can do to help with that. She's so young.

Which is why it seems serendipitous when I see Victoria at PetStop. She smiles at me, remembering my name. No Maltese with her today, and she's got a lab coat on, glasses perched on her head, coffee cup in hand.

"How's the pup doing?" she asks, reaching down to pet Maverick, though her gaze stays on me.

"Fantastic," I answer. "What about your dog?"

"She wasn't mine," she says casually.

I give her a weird look.

"Long story."

My hand is resting on the pig's ears. She tosses a treat from her pocket into the cart. "That's on the house," she says with a smile. "And if you're still up for coffee, my lunch break is in fifteen minutes."

"Yeah…sure. Things didn't work out with the other guy?" It seems like this should be assumed, but it feels safest to ask.

"No, I'm just cheating," she says, without skipping a beat.

I take in a breath before I realize she's teasing.

And then I start to put things together. "The dog was his," I say.

"Yes," she answers.

"I'm sorry," I say.

"Don't be," she replies. "It's what happens when a relationship goes down in flames. And when I go down, I like for it to be in flames."

I want to ask what happened, but I just say, "I'll meet you at the coffee shop in fifteen then. Outside or inside?" I glance at Maverick. Victoria does too.

"On this perfect day? Outside."

I smile. "Want me to order something for you?"

"Sure," she says. "Hook me up with a double espresso."

"Intense," I say.

"That's me. Also, I'm a total addict." She nods to the coffee cup already in her hand. "I try to stop at three so it doesn't wreck my sleep. On nights I want to sleep anyway." She laughs.

I laugh too.

And our mini-date is just more of that. I insist on paying for her coffee even though she tries to pay me back. I'm not sure if that's what makes an official date or not, but if it does, then it's a small price for making it official.

"So when did you know you wanted to be a vet?" I ask.

"I was finished with my undergrad by age twenty," she says. "My dad said he'd pay for medical school or nothing. I chose a vet school the next week."

"Gutsy," I say. "So you took the loss?"

"Nah, Daddy still paid for it," she says. "He's all talk."

I nod like I understand, though I don't.

"I haven't let him regret it. I take him to Vegas every year for Father's Day as a thank you."

"Sounds like you roll high."

She laughs.

"You have no idea."

I don't. By age twenty-three I still didn't even know what I wanted to do with my life and was working odd jobs and wasting my time in random college classes. It was a whole other year for me before I took my first EMT class and got myself hooked. Then a year working before I decided to take the plunge into paramedic school.

That was the first time I found any real purpose in my career life. I'd worked for half a dozen fast food companies, one grocery store, one furniture store, and spent a summer roofing. I'd taken math classes, science classes, one disaster of a European literature class (whatever remains of my GPA is probably still hurting from that).

But when I first rode in the ambulance I realized I was good at it—good at driving fast, good at reacting fast in an emergency, good at thinking fast through the sequence of events that needed to happen in order to make whatever the disaster was less disastrous.

I was even good at being nice to crazy people, calming family members, navigating grumpy nurses and helping old ladies at nursing homes. Up to that point, I'd been good at a few non-popular sports (wrestling anyone?), decent at school (European lit excepted), horrible at cleaning the bathroom, and that kind of felt like who I was.

She nudges the cream in my direction. "What are you thinking about over there?"

I shake my head. "Just my job."

"Which is?" she asks.

"Oh, paramedic."

"Mmmm, sexy," she says.

I laugh. Because it one hundred percent isn't. It's a lot of old ladies and poop and drunk people, and then some sad stuff.

"And a great starting place to get experience if you want to move up the ladder to the ER. I could see you in a lab coat. Doctor Lance."

"Now it just sounds like a character on a soap opera," I say.

She laughs. "Told you. Sexy."

I do my best to give her a soap opera doctor smolder. My best, incidentally, is not very good. And just at that moment, an older couple walks past, giving me a strange look.

"Yeah," I say. "Maybe I better stick to just paramedic."

She smiles. "So you're good at moving fast?" There's no denying that she's better at smoldering than I am.

"I guess you could say that," I reply.

"Perfect," she replies. "So am I."

I'm not quite sure we're talking about the same thing, but we plan on lunch tomorrow since I've got to work tonight.

"How's her foot doing?" she asks, glancing down at Maverick.

"Good," I answer, "still a bit of a limp." When I look at Victoria, I feel Becca's face trying to edge into my mind. I push it away—Becca's clearly not interested, and Victoria clearly is.

"Limping, huh? You sure they set it right?"

The question catches me off guard. I mean, no, I'm not sure. I hadn't even thought about it. "They really didn't set it, actually. She had a piece of metal stuck in it and they, uh, took it out."

"Hmmm," she says. "And they're sure it wasn't

broken? Was it in the bone? Did that heal well? Did they take an X-ray?"

My honest answer is that I have no idea, but I don't say that.

Victoria leans over, holding out a hand for her paw.

I'm somewhat surprised when Maverick obediently puts her paw into Victoria's palm. Maybe that's what it means to be alpha. Victoria feels along the ridges of sinews of her leg and Maverick winces, trying to draw the paw back at a certain point.

"It feels okay," she says. "Though it's definitely a little tender. Hopefully not a lingering pocket of infection. You might want to bring her back and have them do a quick check. Or bring her in to me," she says in a no-pressure kind of way, but I feel a little pressure.

When I get home, I call Dr. Reynolds' office to ask if a limp at this point is still normal. Becca answers the phone and I find myself getting a little tongue-tied at her voice.

"Hey," I say, flustered. Isn't there another person who gets the phones; where is she? "This is Lance

Patterson. Um, my dog, Maverick, she's still walking with a bit of a limp and, um…Do you think she maybe needs an X-ray or something? Maybe more antibiotics?"

"Poor girl," Becca says. "She's still limping?"

"A little," I say. "It's not bad. She plays and everything. It's just still…"

"…there," Becca finishes for me. "I can schedule you an appointment if you'd like."

"Sure," I say. "That would be great."

"You have to realize, though, that sometimes healing from a trauma takes time. It could be just nothing. Or at least there's nothing anyone can do something about."

Victoria seemed to think that she could, but I don't say that.

"I just thought it'd be good to check."

"Yeah, sure," Becca says. "Let me get you down. We actually just had a cancellation for tomorrow afternoon. Would that work?"

"Absolutely," I say, relieved they can get her in so quickly.

Until I remember I'm supposed to have a date with Victoria.

"Uh, what time?" I ask.

"Three. Last appointment we have for the next week."

I pause.

"Will that work?" she asks, a little lilt of concern to her voice.

"Yeah," I say quickly. "Yeah, that will work."

CHAPTER 13

Turns out Victoria is way more intense than a double espresso.

She shows up at lunch in a tight shirt and some power heels. I'm not quite sure which message the heels are meant to send—"Watch out, buddy" or "Look at these legs." Both work pretty effectively.

She orders a martini while we wait, talks a mile a minute, and leans over to tell me, "You got the coffee. This one's on me."

By the time we're seated, I know that not only did she graduate by the time she was twenty, but she did it at Brown, with a double major in biology and zoology—neither of them a walk in the park. She's dated two Kennedy relatives, the son of a Hollywood director, and one forty-year-old hotel tycoon. "None of them for more than three months," she laughs. "They can never keep up."

"And what would they have to do in order to keep up?" I ask, leaning forward to enjoy her eyes from a closer range.

"Just speed," she says. "All the speed. Think you can keep up, Ambulance Boy?"

"I'm not sure," I reply, leaning back and letting her lean in this time.

She does, lips twitching at the corners. I realize I'm watching them.

"I'm just a Kentucky boy at heart. Slow talk, slow walk." Also slow at choosing my career, at making certain choices, but I leave that part out of the repartee.

"Slow," she asks. "Or smooth? There's a difference, you know."

I do not, but I just laugh.

"How do you keep from going insane?" I ask when she finishes telling me about how she set up the partnership with PetStop.

"I'm so glad you asked," she replies. "I take Crossfit a few times a week, do my Peloton the others."

"When?"

"4:00 am."

"Of course."

"Of course," she says with a smile. And that smile. Like a cheetah. All the smooth and all the speed.

I order steak; she gets sushi. We laugh. We lean. We cat. We mouse.

In light of our conversation—you know, the Peloton and everything—I'm not expecting her to light up a cigarette when we get to the parking lot, but that's exactly what she does.

I try not to react, but I must give a sort of look because she smiles, the smoke burning at my nostrils.

"Told you I was an addict," she says.

But then we were talking about coffee. And yeah, yeah, I know people smoke, especially in tobacco country. No judgment or whatever. But she's just so devoted, the smoke coming out of her mouth and nose. And the thing is, my dad used to smoke every time I drove in the car with him. And it made me carsick and he never cared. Never even opened the window to let the smoke out.

"You want one?" she asks.

"No thanks," I say. "Used to make me carsick when my dad smoked."

And just like him, she doesn't bother to stamp it out.

"It relaxes me," she says.

I nod, and we walk to my car. "Hey," she says, glancing at her Mercedes. "Since you've got to work tonight, why don't we head over to my house to watch a movie right now. We can take my car."

"That would be awesome," I say, "but I might have to take a raincheck." I glance at my car and Maverick plants her face solidly against the window, leaving a drool mark. "I made an appointment with the vet this afternoon. It was the only time they could get her in."

Victoria frowns. "You should have brought her in to me sometime. I could have taken care of it at a more convenient time."

"I just thought the continuity of care," I say.

And then she smiles like there was never a frown. "That totally makes sense. I'm just disappointed we can't spend more time together."

"Me too," I say, but something in my gut feels suddenly a little unsure of that.

Maverick is whining through the crack I've left in the window. I unlock the door and let her out to do her business. Slow, not smooth.

"What about Sunday?" she asks. "I've got the day off, a nice empty apartment, and a couple bottles of Chardonnay."

And, I mean, I might not like cigarette smoke, but I'm still a dude. "I, um, I work the night before, but after noon should work. I'll give you a call."

"Do," she says, turning to walk toward her car. The strap of her tank top slips down off her shoulder when she does, and she doesn't reach up to fix it.

I shake off the image, as well as any lingering cigarette smell. It feels confusing.

Maverick is unconcerned about everything that just happened. She seems to favor asphalt as the place to do her business and leaves a bit of a puddle before I realize what's happening.

"Girl," I moan. But I guess it's just as well since by now we're running late, and we've got to move quickly. Quickly. I get the feeling Victoria has mistaken my job as a sign of my speed. And I am fast when I'm on a call, with an impending disaster. I'm just not sure that's what I want my love life to look like too.

When I arrive at the Dr. Reynolds' office, it feels a little like showing up on my mom's porch after my first mildly unsuccessful semester at college. Comforting. The paintings of flowers on the walls, the soft blue paint, milky gray tiling. Yes, please.

Becca glances at the clock when I arrive and I realize I'm late. It's starting to feel like I'm the only kid in town who's slow, not smooth.

"I got held over at lunch," I reply.

She shrugs. "No worries. Dr. Reynolds wouldn't turn you away even if you'd spent your time making out with her competition."

And as far as I know, there's no reason on earth that Becca would know that I just had lunch with another veterinarian. She doesn't even say it with that passive-aggressive dig it seems like she should have if she'd known, but my neck gets hot.

Becca gives me a funny look, then glances down at Maverick. "How's the leg?"

"It's fine," I answer. "It's just…a friend was looking at it and wondered if there was an infection at the healing point."

Her eyebrow moves up a notch. "What friend?"

"Just," I begin, "it doesn't matter. Anyway, I was just wondering if there's anything to that."

Dr. Reynolds pops her head out as I say it. "Bring in that little darling."

And I do, Becca trailing after.

I leave with a sample of anti-inflammatory. Doctor Reynolds says it doesn't look like an infection.

When Becca hands me my paperwork, she walks over to the carrier and looks into Maverick's eyes, reaching in to touch a paw. "Maybe this sounds weird," she begins. "But I've been taking this anatomy class, and volunteering for a couple PTs in town. I think I might know an exercise that could help her."

"Don't you think the anti-inflammatory will do that?" I ask.

"If it's just inflammation and *if* it goes away," she answers.

"You don't think it is."

"I just thought maybe a little rehab might do her good." She smiles in a way that turns down, not up. "But you're right, it was a weird idea."

"I mean, if you think it would help."

"I don't know what I think," she says, that strange smile still stuck to her face. I want to reach out, touch a cheek, lift it up a bit.

"It couldn't hurt," I say. "What do you think would help?"

The next pet comes through the door—a Siamese who looks like it's just about scratched through its carrier. Becca throws her smile that direction. "Hello, Mrs. Anderson. Have a seat and Dr. Reynolds will be with you shortly."

Turning back to me, she hands me my paperwork. "I don't have time to show you right now, but I could some other time."

"Maybe Sunday afternoon," I say. "I usually visit my mom, but I could go there later."

"I don't want to keep you from your mom," she says. "I'm not a monster. And who knows what the consequences might be of keeping her waiting."

"Consequences?" I say and laugh.

"My mom would be ticked if I told her I was skipping a visit to do doggy rehab."

I don't know why the comment surprises me. Maybe because I'm pretty sure that if my mom knew there was a girl involved she'd want me to double up on the doggy rehab. "Yeah, my mom's pretty chill," I reply.

"Must be nice," Becca grumbles.

"Yours isn't?"

"Don't get me wrong," Becca says. "My mom's amazing, but the woman has a schedule to keep and if you're on it, you'd best not miss out."

Reminds me slightly of Victoria, and just like that I remember that my Sunday was kind of spoken for.

"Don't keep your mom waiting," Becca is saying as I try to work out the details in my head. "Where does she live anyway?"

"She just moved from the Swallowsville Rehab Center and is back at her house."

Becca's eyebrow quirks up into that perfect line. "I was expecting something like, 'the north side.' What happened?"

"Stroke," I say shortly, not wanting to talk about it. "And honestly, you're right, Sunday might not work out well."

"I'm sorry," she adds. "That must suck for her."

"She's a decent sport about it actually."

"Doesn't mean it doesn't suck," Becca says.

"Yeah," I reply, looking into those blue blue eyes. I notice that they're lined with a ring of darker blue, and that right now they match the rest of her face, no mask. "It doesn't."

"Well, here's my number," she says, texting it to me. I realize she's had my info all the time on her computer. "If you have time, maybe I could have a look at Maverick—strange as it is. I just have a little hunch that one of her ligaments might be a little tight. If she could fix that…Yeah, I sound crazy."

"No," I say. "I mean, mildly. But I think it's a good idea." My phone pings with her text. Her number, this thing I've tried to get a couple times. Right there in my hand. But now I'm kind of dating someone else.

Maverick is sniffing at my shirt, and Becca leans in. The cigarette smoke. I feel an illogical sense of panic. "I was at lunch," I say. "Someone was smoking. She must smell it."

Becca nods. I want her to say, "Hey, call me sometime." But she doesn't, just hands me the bill.

I sigh and take it, opening one eye, afraid of what I'm going to see. Then both eyes pop open. "This is wrong," I say. It says I'm all paid up.

"It's not wrong," Becca answers, not even looking up from her computer.

I stuff the paper into my pocket. "Hey, tell Dr. Reynolds thank you."

"Will do," she says.

Maverick whines when we leave, like she wants to stay with the pretty lady who smells like strawberries and not Marlboros.

CHAPTER 14

"So…" Macie, one of my best friends, says when I tell her. "He's a paramedic who saved a puppy and visits his infirm mother every Sunday." She snags a chip from the bowl at the tiniest Mexican restaurant ever and heaps on a generous dose of salsa.

"He should probably visit more," Gretchen says, swirling the lemon in her drink. "You need to find out if he visits more."

"You need to marry him," Macie says, popping the chip in her mouth.

"You're one to talk," I shoot back.

"Hey," Gretchen begins. "You know she's sensitive that Tad hasn't popped the question yet."

"I am not," Macie says, going for another chip—a sure sign that she is.

"Are too," I counter. "But none of this is the point, and I guarantee you'll have a proposal by Christmas, so relax."

"Enough about me," Macie says. "That man is a catch."

Like she's the official matchmaker since she's the only one who has a real boyfriend.

"He's a guy," I say. "With junk and secrets and who knows what. He was late today because he was at lunch, and he smelled like cigarette smoke even though I guarantee he doesn't smoke and…" I trail off.

"He was on a date," Gretchen says. The waiter arrives with a plate of steaming fajita fillings.

"I think he's seeing this other veterinarian in town," I say.

"The plot thickens," Gretchen replies.

"Doesn't it though."

The waiter puts my burrito in front of me, hands Macie her salad.

"How's class?" Macie asks and I know that I must start to glow because both of my friends grin. I tell them about ligaments and bones and skin.

"Who knew you were such a nerd?" Macie says.

"When we first met, I just thought you were a tramp."

"Uh, thanks for that," I say. "To be fair, when you put your date's hot bod in that Uber, I couldn't have guessed *you* were a genius."

"I can't decide if that's a compliment or insult," Macie replies.

"It's clearly both," Gretchen says, filling a fajita. "Now let Becca continue."

"My anatomy professor was telling me about this research opportunity we would do together," I continue, forgetting about my food for a second.

"You know what that means in angst-y B movies," Gretchen replies.

"That my professor is going to try to get me into bed?" I say.

"Of course. Maybe you don't need puppy boy," Gretchen says.

Macie rolls her eyes.

"Except that I'm way too old for angst. And that professor is a straight woman, so research with her seems like a safe, passion-free bet."

"How dull," Gretchen says, reaching over for a bit of my burrito. I swat her away.

"Are you going to do the research project?" Macie

asks. "It's probably a huge time commitment. Will you have to cut back at work?"

I feel the little worry lines pop up along my forehead.

"Becca's worrying about her sister more than work," Gretchen says, making another grab for my food.

"I am not," I shoot back, although I'm worrying about *exactly* that—if I cut back the hours I usually use to help Sally Mae, that'd leave plenty for a little research.

Gretchen smiles.

"Okay, I am a little," I say.

"I know you love your family," Macie says. "But you can't let that make your decision for you."

I nod, but Macie doesn't really get it. After all, she's a bit of an orphan—her dad died when she was young, and her mom passed just a couple years after she graduated, so what does she know about family obligations?

"Your income, however," Macie is saying. "I'm not sure you should cut back at work."

"Income schmincome," Gretchen replies. "She could probably make up for it by joining my Glossies team and selling lipstick. Look at it on her."

"No argument," Macie replies.

My cuteness strikes again. "I don't really want to sell lipstick," I say softly.

"I know," Gretchen replies, taking my hand. "It was mostly a joke, but if you do need some cash, it's there."

"What DO you want to do?" Macie asks.

I want to change the world, I think, but instead I answer, "I don't know."

Macie looks unconvinced. She's becoming more of a detective every day.

CHAPTER 15

I'm slipping into my shoes to head to Victoria's when Mom calls me, crying.

"Are you okay?" I ask, grabbing my keys.

"I burned the cheese," she sniffles, "and the milk curdled."

I'm practically dragging Maverick outside so she can do her business, and the words don't sink in at first.

"Are you hurt?" I ask, trying to put it together.

"The casserole is ruined," she says.

Maverick looks at me—one eye foggy as usual, but the other one brown and deep. She can hear Mom crying.

"Mom," I say. "Are you hurt?"

"No," she says. "I just tried to make a casserole—a

casserole I've made a thousand times in your life, your favorite casserole—" She chokes up again. "But these stupid hands won't do it."

"Don't call them stupid," I say, just like she used to when I was young and learning to play baseball.

"A million times," she repeats.

"Listen, why don't I come over a little earlier today? I'll stop at the store on the way, grab some fresh ingredients." Victoria's face flashes through my mind, but that shouldn't be a problem. I'll just bring her with me. We can watch the movie after.

"I wanted to have it done when you came over tonight."

"I'll come now, Mom. We'll do it together."

She sniffles and my heart clenches up.

"That would be nice, honey," she says.

"See you soon, Mom."

"Love you, hon."

"Love you, too."

When I hang up the phone, I realize I didn't mention that I'd be bringing a date. And why didn't I tell her? It would have made Mom's day.

I pick up the phone, take a breath like I'm bracing for something. Before I can worry too much about what, I hit the V that I've got in for Victoria. Just a brief change of plans. No big deal. Plus, she can meet my mom. We'll watch the movie later. Win win. Right? *Right,* I ask myself again.

Wrong.

"Your mom?" Victoria says, like I'm an eighteen-year-old living in the basement, not a full-grown adult helping his mom out.

"I mean, yeah," I say. "She had a stroke, and sometimes she has trouble with things. I was going to go after the movie, but thought maybe we could swing by before instead."

"You were going to go afterwards?" Victoria says. "You were planning to come to my house, watch a movie and that's it, and then go to your mom's house for dinner."

I'm not sure what to say in response. Clearly, Victoria had more planned than a movie. And it seems like maybe I should have anticipated that, been eager for that. But right now, I just want to get Maverick in the car and go buy broccoli for my mom. Is that weird? Is it as sad as Victoria's making it sound?

"She's my mom," I say lamely.

"Yeah," Victoria says, drawing out the word.

"You don't need to come," I say. "Maybe I could come by afterwards?"

The silence on the other end is answer enough.

"Or not," I say.

"Yeah, maybe not," she says. And that's it. At least it's clear.

I load Maverick into the car and head to the store, feeling like I should be mad, hurt, indignant, embarrassed…something. But as I grab cheese, broccoli, and a quart of milk, I realize that the only feeling washing over me is relief.

By the time I get back in the car, I'm smiling. "Guess it's just you and me again," I say to Maverick. "Hope Mom's happy with a doggy grandbaby."

Maverick nuzzles a wet nose against my hand, brushing the arm with that perfect, soft ear. She, at least, is happy to go help my mom. Sounds like the perfect woman to me.

CHAPTER 16

BECCA

The drive to Sally Mae's is like a drive to a fairy kingdom. Trees that canopy a narrow, winding road. At this time of year, with the sun high, they cast a green hue on the road and everything around. Butterflies flit along the wild-flowers. Deer, rabbits, birds.

Sally's house is even better—a natural pond out back where she keeps ducks, who share the pond with several wild duck families as well. The chicken coop is nicer than my apartment, and belongs on the cover of *Farm Queen* magazine. If there is no *Farm Queen* magazine, then someone should create it just to feature Sally's coop. Not to mention the chickens —some are the basic varieties, but she's got a ton of crested and rare breeds as well. Once you wander past the coop, you come to the rabbit cage. Though cage hardly seems a fair word. Quarters, maybe.

Stables with their four horses, a small red barn with a few cats. A goat to eat the weeds and provide her with milk. Two dogs, Henry and Edward, that greet me as I come up the drive. And one princess of a housecat, who eats from a bowl and sleeps on a pillow, and is lovingly brushed every day by Sally's oldest daughter.

As soon as I open the car door, Edward shoves his head in (Henry waits more demurely to the side). I can't help but think about Maverick, and then Lance. I clamber out of my car and give Edward a good rub down, trying to push my thoughts away. I try thinking about the property—the new shed that Sally just built, and then my research—a study of ligaments, especially those in the upper body.

But Lance keeps creeping back into my thoughts. I tell myself it's because I'm wondering if maybe Maverick has a tight ligament causing that limp. I hold Edward's paw like we're shaking. He gives me a dog smile, then tries to lick my face.

"Oh, nice try," I say. "I know Sally's taught you not to kiss people on the lips."

And then I'm back to thinking about Lance. Bad brain.

This time I tell myself it's because I still think he'd be the perfect story for Sally's channel. What angle could they take that wouldn't be offensive to someone hurt in an accident? They could leave out the human patients altogether. Which sounds a little awful when I think about it. But that's story, right?

Henry has trotted over for his part in the action and I'm scratching his back. He's gotten old, and sometimes limps from a little arthritis. Could *that* be Maverick's problem? Then I'm back to thinking about Lance.

As I walk up Sally's pathway (it's lined on either side with roses, in case you were thinking it was a normal sidewalk to a normal house), I wonder if maybe I'm thinking about him because here we are doing the same thing—him going to his mom's for dinner, and me to mine. Only he's going because he wants to, even though his mom is recovering from a stroke, and I'm going because I have to, even though my family is healthy and strong and ten thousand percent capable.

I stand at Sally's door—rounded at the top like the opening to a cottage, painted blue with a little window at the top—and go over potential dinner conversation ideas in my head. It's something I do every week. And who does that, rehearses what they're going to say to their sister and their mother —both of whom they see every week?

I settle on a discussion of one-eared kittens and knock on the door (there's a knocker in case you thought I'd have to use my fist). We've had three one-eared kittens come into the office this week, and there's something so adorable about them. Two of the cats were hardcore fighters, and one was a sweet little adolescent female, who really shouldn't be left as an outdoor cat.

I hear the clamor of Sally's kids: Ben and Geraldine. "Aunt Becca!" they screech.

I open my arms to catch them both in a huge hug, then sniff. "Smells like Grandma's been hard at work."

"Grandma's always hard at work," Geri says, giggling.

Truer words were never spoken.

"And is Grandpa here too?"

"Grandma's making him set the table," Ben says. "Good thing too, because otherwise it would have been us."

"There are worse things than setting the table," I whisper back, conspiratorially. "You could have to dry the dishes."

Geri rolls her eyes. "No one dries them, Aunt

Becca. The dishwasher does that."

"Not when I was a kid," I say.

Snowball, the princess cat, pads into the room—both her ears looking lovely and full. And then I know that my discussion topic for dinner is way too boring. But it's all I've got.

It's not enough.

Not even close.

"Becca," Sally calls from a spiral stairway that leads to her office. "Glad you're here." My niece and nephew scatter—worried, I'm sure, that they'll be given a job if she discovers them. "Hey, do you have those edits done? I've been waiting all week."

I'm honestly not sure what she's talking about at first. I've been working, doing school, adding in research. "Edits?" I ask.

"Oh no," Sally says, running a hand through her hair and stalking into the dining room.

I follow. Mom is wearing an apron that says, "I mean business," which looks like not a single drop of food has ever been spilled on it. Dusting her clean hands onto it, she moves into the kitchen.

"Remind me," I say to Sally. "What edits?"

"The edits," she says. "For the show. The ones I asked you to do, told you I'd pay you a competitive rate. Remember?"

A foggy conversation from the week before fights its way into my memory.

"Did I agree to do them?" I ask.

"You said to send them over and you'd have a look."

"So I *didn't* agree to do them," I respond. I mean, truly, it doesn't sound like much of a contract to me.

"Come on, Becca. It's okay if you forgot, but don't pretend you didn't agree to do them."

"But, like, did I?" I ask. "Because it sounds like you wanted me to do them, and I wasn't sure about it, and I said I'd have a look."

Mom pops her head out like she's going to intervene, but Sally holds up a hand, and Mom disappears back into the kitchen.

"Okay," Sally says, leveling a look at me—a look I know, a look that says I just lost this fight. "Did you have a look?"

"Where'd you send them?"

"A file to your email."

Which I know I should check, but with my classes started, things got away from me. "I'm sorry," I say. "I didn't look. I've mostly only been checking my school email."

Sally throws her hands in the air. "Great. I need that ready to go by Tuesday." And then there's this pause. And the thing is, I know what the pause means. I'm supposed to say my part of the script. *Oh my gosh, Sally. I'm so sorry. I'll get it to you as soon as possible.* But even though I know my lines, I find myself not saying them.

The pause lengthens. Finally Sally says, "I was going to pay you."

And I know it's true. She would have paid me, and generously.

But instead of my correct line, I find myself saying, "Maybe I don't want to be paid."

"You want to do it for free?" Sally asks.

"I don't want to do it at all." The script is burning, right in front of my eyes.

"But you need the money," she says, like there was never another reason in the world for doing a thing.

"Not really," I say. "I actually don't *need* the money. I have a job."

"A job that barely pays the rent. And what about your classes? How are you paying for them?"

"I got a scholarship," I say.

She looks at me sideways. "Nice of you to mention that."

"Honestly, Sally, why would I need to mention it? It's my life, my money. I'm thirty-one years old."

"Exactly," Sally says. "And look what you've done with yourself. You've had every minimum wage job under the sun. So that you could settle for working a low-paying job as an assistant and taking night classes about who knows what. Will those classes even lead you anywhere? If so, where?"

And here I realize just how tricky it is to deviate from the script.

I open my mouth to give an answer, but I don't have one. *Will* the classes lead me anywhere? I don't know. I mean, I had hoped so, but I have to admit that I don't really have a specific, carefully mapped career path in mind. Somewhere interesting. Somewhere wonderful. Is that what I should say to my sister? Definitely not.

Will they lead me to veterinary school? I mean, I guess maybe they could, but I realize that somehow I intentionally chose at least one class that wouldn't, at least one class that would be utterly useless if I wanted to become a vet. Human Anatomy. The class where I'm really shining, the class where I've been asked to do research on something as simple and basic as human ligaments.

"This editing job," Sally Mae is saying, grabbing onto my silence. "It could do more than pay the bills. It would give you plenty of money—enough for more than night classes at the community college. And it could launch you into so many other things you could do. It could give you something for your resume if you wanted to freelance, or work in marketing. And if you just want to study animals, it could pay for your classes without you having to stress about it."

"I wasn't stressed," I say. And then before I can stop myself, "And I don't want to study animals. I want to study people. Or cells. Or maybe even chemistry. But I don't want to be a vet. I don't want a career with animals at all. Even though if I had one, that would also benefit you with your home farm-menagerie-cottage." Outside, a rooster crows right on cue. "Like every single job you suggest and think would be 'perfect' for me does."

"You're not serious," Sally Mae says. "You really think that the thing that's motivating me to offer you a job, to encourage you to become a vet, is my own needs?"

I mean, I hadn't really thought about it until now. But actually, yes, I do. At least a little. "It sure seems that way."

"You know I could hire someone else for less than I was going to pay you," she snaps. "I was trying to do you—YOU—a favor."

"Well," I say. "You can stop trying. Because I don't want your favors. Or your advice."

"Well, too bad," Sally says. "Because my advice is this. Find something to do with your life. Something that will do more than pay the bills. If you're even really accomplishing that."

"Thanks for that," I say, chewing on my thoughts before I spit them out. "And here's my advice for you. Find someone else who actually cares about editing and hire her."

My stomach is grumbling and Dad is edging his way out to set the roast on the table. He looks back and forth between us. I turn to leave anyway. I can get a burger somewhere. I can live without all this.

I spend the rest of the afternoon driving around town, past places where we spent our childhoods.

The pond we lived near when we were small— the place Sally found a duckling that she saved and then raised. The petting zoo where our parents used to take us. The farm where we would come on Saturdays for horse riding lessons. Our high school where Sally started a program that matched families with pets for the local humane society—she had a table she set up every Friday with applications.

Then I drive past the humane society itself. A few people are out front with signs rallying for something. I squint—a no-kill shelter.

I wouldn't be surprised if Sally had started that campaign too, except if she did, it would be more than signs. It would be action. She'd be out there raising money to make it happen. Or she'd adopt all the animals herself, and start her own darn shelter. That was how Sally did. Animal after animal after animal.

At the end, I stop at the dog park, just sitting in my car, watching the animals with their owners. It's not that I don't like animals. I *love* animals. It's just that I don't want that to be the one thing that defines me forever and ever. And Sally Mae does. She is happy for it to define her, and maybe because she's so happy about it, she wants it to define me as well. I guess I can understand that. What I can't understand is why she can't cut me free of it. She'd never trap a hawk and keep it to herself; why does she want to trap me?

Something smacks up against the window and I practically jump out of my skin.

When I glance left, I'm surprised to see a doggy

face pressed against the glass, and I can't help but laugh. It's Maverick, and she's getting drool everywhere. Lance is doing his best to haul her back, and barely succeeding. Finally, he just picks her up, and she must be putting on some weight because his arms get a definite flex when he lifts and I catch myself staring at them, and then shake myself out of it. I open the door.

"Hey," he says, setting Maverick back down and blocking her, so she can't jump up again as I make my way out of the car. "Sorry about that. Maverick recognized you before I did."

"Dogs are good at that," I say, squatting down to pet her.

"Everything okay?" he asks.

"Oh, yeah," I say. "Why?" *Do I not look okay?*

"I just thought you had dinner with your family on Sundays," he says.

"Oh, yeah," I answer. "Tonight something came up so it didn't work out." I glance again at Maverick. "And I thought you had dinner with *your* mother on Sunday."

He steps to the side, and this older woman wobbles forward. She's a solid foot shorter than Lance. Late sixties maybe, or early seventies—older than my mom by about a decade. With that silver hair that's in vogue, ice blue eyes, and…part of her mouth hanging down, a cheek that seems a little lower than the other. "Oh, hello," she says to me, like she's having the best day of her life.

"Mom, this is Rebecca," Lance says. "She works at the vet office where I take Maverick."

"Just Becca," I say, extending a hand.

"Janet," she says, then takes my hand in a soft handshake. "It's wonderful to meet you, dear."

I'm not sure my own mother has ever called anyone 'dear' in her life. "It's nice to meet you too," I say. Then to Lance, "Post dinner walk?"

"Actually we just decided to come out while the casserole bakes. Mom insists we bake it on low heat. She says that keeps the chicken moist. And Maverick gets antsy."

"I bet she does," I say, squatting down to pet those glorious ears again. "All those yummy chicken smells she can't have."

Lance's mother clears her throat.

"Speaking of chicken," Lance says. "Have you eaten?"

My stomach growls right then, traitor that it is. "Oh, uh, no, not yet. But that's okay. You don't have to feed me."

"Dear," his mother—Janet—says. "It would be our

pleasure. You have no idea how dull it gets with just the two of us."

"Doesn't look dull at all," I say, smiling. "Plus, you've got Maverick."

"Well, she does keep it interesting," Janet says.

"But seriously, you should come," Lance adds. "Mom made an *enormous* casserole."

"Are you sure?" I ask, and Maverick puts a gentle paw on my shin, like she's begging, too.

Lance and his mother both laugh at the same time. This unified laugh that is the most beautiful, remarkable thing I've ever heard.

"You can't say 'no' to Maverick," Lance says.

"No, I guess I can't," I reply.

"Good girl," Janet says, leaning down to pet her head.

D inner is completely delicious. Simple, homey, amazing. I wonder if Janet's ever tried making sushi or saag or Pad Thai or tempura or any of the wild stuff my mom has tried. Or if she just does comfort food. Which she does very well.

"I'm stuffed," I say when we're done.

"But you hardly ate a thing," Janet says. "We'll

have to send you home with a plate."

"I would love that," I say honestly, not even bothering to politely decline.

Janet beams.

"Do you work tomorrow?" Janet asks Lance, and I realize it's the first time anyone's mentioned work.

"Yup," Lance says.

I find myself leaning in, hoping for a story of some kind.

"Do you know Lance found Maverick on a call?" his mother asks.

"I, uh, did know that."

From the look on Lance's face, I can tell that he's begging me not to tell the story of him fibbing about it at first. That's fair, because I think I've got a look on my face begging him not to tell the story of me accusing him of hitting Maverick with his car.

"He's got a bunch of other stories too," Janet says mischievously, "but I've heard them all. You two should go for a walk and talk. I'll watch Maverick."

"Maverick could probably come if we went for a walk. Look, she's already heard the word."

Maverick was, in fact, running toward the door where her leash was hanging on a hook.

"But I guess you knew that already, didn't you?" Lance says to his mother in a mock accusatory tone.

And suddenly I get it. She said the word so we'd have to go on a walk. Maverick would demand it.

Well played, Janet. Well played.

"I'm really sorry about that," Lance says as soon as we're out the door. "You do *not* have to come for a walk with us if you don't want to."

I shrug, trying to hide the fact that I'm actually really happy to be here, on a walk with the two of them.

"For real," Lance says. "I can take you back to the dog park. Thanks for coming tonight. It really made Mom's day."

Your *mom's*, I want to ask. Not *yours?* Instead, I say, "So she's trying to hook you up?"

"Always," he says, laughing. "It's her total thing."

"And your dad?" I ask. "Has he, uh, passed?"

"Passed?" Lance says, and then realizes. "Nope. He's still alive and kicking. They're divorced."

"Oh, sorry," I say. "Your mom just seemed so domestic. I guess I just figured..."

"They were married for all of eleven months. Then I arrived and messed things up. At least in my dad's opinion. Mom worked till the day of her stroke."

"Really?" I ask. "What did she do?"

"Engineer," he answers.

And I admit, I'm surprised. She tricked me with that soft handshake and the casserole and the everything.

"She was really good at it, too," Lance says. "Age is a beast."

Is it? I consider my parents with their jobs, Sally Mae. It feels like they'll go forever. And here I am doing…nothing really. Just jumping around with different jobs, like Sally Mae said. What if I get to seventy and realize it really was all a waste?

"But your dad's still healthy?" I ask.

"Sure," he says.

"And his job? Or is he retired?"

"Oh no," Lance answers. "Still working. Law. He's good at what he does, too."

It's all he says before switching the conversation back to his mother. A couple of times he looks at me kind of sideways like he wants to ask me about mine.

Then it's my turn to change topics. We talk about our favorite music, first cars, first dates, worst dates.

He tells me he didn't bomb at college (except an

English class, apparently), but nothing there felt really right until he found EMS. I tell him I didn't even attempt more than a semester of college. "Until now," I say.

"Really?" he asks, slowing.

"Yeah," I say. "Guess I'm a little late to the party."

"It's not late," he says. "If now is when you want to start, then you're right on time."

I smile. "Well, that's up for debate, but thank you."

He gives me a funny look on the debate part. "So what are you studying?"

"Ah, the golden question," I reply. "I'm taking an anatomy class and a bio class."

"A science girl, huh?" he says.

It does not escape my notice that he doesn't ask again about a specific major. I appreciate that.

We wind our way through his mother's neighborhood until I notice we've made our way back to the dog park, and my car. I catch myself feeling a little disappointed about that.

We pause at my door, him looking down into my face. The lopsided smile. "Glad we bumped into you," he says.

"Me too," I reply.

There's this little pause, my face tilted up to his.

"See you around, Becca." And then he turns and begins to walk away, Maverick sniffing and trotting alongside him.

"Hey, Lance," I say.

He pauses, pivots.

My mouth feels dry and tight, like I've just stepped way out of my zone. "Do you want to maybe…?"

He takes a step toward me and then laughs. "Once you've had one dinner with my mother, you can never get enough. Right?"

I kind of giggle, hide it with my hand. As though I'm really becoming a twenty-year-old college kid (or maybe a thirteen-year-old junior high kid).

"But maybe, if you'd like, we could even go out to dinner *without* my mom some time."

I swallow. "I would like that."

"I'll call you," he says. Maverick is tugging at the leash, and he turns away again.

I open my car door. He will call, right? That's not just a thing people say? I mean, sometimes it's what people say. But not this time. I watch them through my rearview window as I turn on my car.

Maverick still has a faint limp and I remember that I was supposed to try to help with that, but I got too caught up in Lance. And how did that happen?

CHAPTER 17

"Well, Mom," I say when I get back. "You're the MVP of team dating."

"Was that ever in doubt?" she asks. "It certainly wasn't going to be you."

I laugh.

"I liked her," Mom says. "Please tell me you got her number and will soon be sweeping her off her feet."

"I already had her number," I say.

Mom lifts her good eyebrow.

"Because we were already friends." Well, sort of.

"And the sweeping her off her feet part?" Mom asks.

"I got it, Mom."

"Take her to a nice place," she continues like she

didn't hear me. "Not some dingy bar. And wear a decent outfit."

I look down.

"You look fine today, hon. But wear something a little more upscale. Like you would for a job interview. Which is what this is, after all."

I snort. "Any more instructions?"

"Oh, dozens," she says. "Be sure to shave. Make yourself smell good. Give a generous tip. Oh, and leave the dog at home. Sorry, sweetie," she says to Maverick.

"What?" I say. "She's my secret weapon."

"You're going to have to learn to win a woman over without an animal. And you're going to take Becca to a nice enough place that Mavvy won't be allowed." She crosses her arms, like this is non-negotiable.

"Fine," I say.

"And bring flowers."

"It's a first date, Mom. I'm not bringing flowers."

She shares a smirk with Maverick, and they both look at me like they're dealing with an amateur.

"They don't have to be roses," Mom says.

I show up with lilies. And I do smell nice, and I did shave. But I'm not dressed for a job interview. Just jeans and a decent shirt. And I keep looking down for Maverick—those sweet, wonky eyes of hers—but she's not there.

Becca is meeting me at the restaurant, which my mother one thousand percent did not approve, but it was Becca's suggestion, and it's not 1980 anymore. It only takes me a minute to see the advantage of picking her up though. Because as it is, she comes up behind me and taps my shoulder, which catches me off guard. So then I whirl around, surprised, and sort of thrust the flowers awkwardly into her hands like they're hot poison and I'm trying to get rid of them. She takes them just as awkwardly, and maybe she smiles, but it's too hard for my brain to keep up.

"Thank you," she says.

And I realize that when you don't pick a woman up at her house, but still give her flowers, she has nothing to do with them, except carry them into the restaurant like we're headed to the prom and forgot our formalwear.

"Do you want me to keep them in the car?" I ask.

"It's a little warm," she says. "I wouldn't want them to wilt. They're beautiful."

I nod, and for a moment we stand, facing each other like it's the end of the date, not the beginning. "Did I make it awkward?" I say after a beat.

"No," she answers. "You made it nice."

Then, as I open the restaurant door for her, she asks with a little mischief in her voice, "Just tell me your mother didn't buy them."

"Nope," I say. "I went to the grocery store like a big boy and made the purchase all on my own."

"Aww," she teases. "You picked them out and everything."

"Sure did," I say, as the crush of the dinner crowd drowns out her laughter and pushes us closer together. I can't say that I mind.

I haven't exactly picked a black-tie location. Just a popular steak place I wanted to try out. Very popular from the looks of it. Becca and I are jostled side to side, then body to body. I swear we're close enough that I can feel her heart, or maybe it's mine. "Wow," I say, leaning down so she can hear me, our faces now nearly close enough to touch. "I didn't realize it'd be this busy."

"It's okay," she replies, her lips almost brushing my ear. "It's kind of fun."

And it is.

A waiter is walking through the packed crowd,

taking drink orders while we wait for our tables. People are popping actual coins into an actual retro jukebox and selecting songs. "Do you want anything?" I ask.

"Honestly, just a water," she answers.

"Ah, a cheap date," I say into her ear. She smells amazing, even in this crowd. Like a spicy flower.

"Only of one sort," she says, with a wink.

"Do I get to figure out which sort?" I ask.

"You already did," she answers.

And then the host calls our name and I touch the small of her back, leading her through the crowd to a little table in the corner. It's still loud, but I couldn't have asked for anything better.

"So what's good?" she asks, leaning over the little table.

"No idea," I answer. "It's my first time here. Just don't ask me to share something."

"Wasn't going to," she answers, her nose in the menu, the right side of her mouth lifted up in this sneaky sort of half smile. I like it.

Someone chooses an old swing song for the jukebox and she taps her fingers. I move my hand nearby and tap along with her. Soon we're tapping together and she's smiling—her eyes fully connected to it. I lean forward, about to say something, when the waiter pops up beside us. I haven't even glanced at the menu.

Becca knows what she wants and I steal a minute to glance through the steak options. "Appetizer?" I ask her.

"I'm good," she says.

"You sure?" I ask.

"I'm a cheap date," she says.

We hand our menus back, and the waiter gives Becca a quick glance before flitting away.

The restaurant has quieted just a little so that we don't have to lean and shout to be heard. Now we can just lean, and I kind of like that.

"You didn't bring your mom," she says, teasingly. "Or Maverick."

"I know," I say. "Now I don't know what to do with myself." It's a little too true.

"Tell me about your job," she says. "It must be wild sometimes."

"Yeah, I mean, definitely sometimes. But sometimes it's really slow, and we just sit there and watch TV or whatever."

"You don't work out like the firefighters?" There's that soft tease to her voice.

"Whatever," I say. "They watch more TV than we

do. Firefighters only have about a quarter of the call volume that we do. *And* they get paid more."

"For real?" she asks.

"For real."

"They also get calendars," she says with an evil glint in her eye.

"Do you have one?" I ask.

"Not at present," she answers. "Why don't you guys get calendars?"

"Just not hot enough," I answer.

"I see," she says coyly.

"Ouch," I answer.

"But for real," she says, "tell me about the weirdest call—with a happy ending—that you've had."

"The weirdest…" I say, thinking.

"With a happy ending," she repeats. "I don't want any death or dismemberment. I honestly don't know how you guys handle it. Part of the reason I don't want to be a vet is because it's too sad to put suffering animals to sleep."

"You don't want to be a vet?" I ask. "But your job?"

"Just a stop gap," she answers. "Like every other job I've had while I try to figure out what I want to do with my life."

"Why not a vet?" I ask.

"I wasn't kidding. I really don't want to see animals suffering and have to put them to sleep. It's so sad to me—both parts. Like a lose, lose situation."

"Yeah, I know what you mean. I don't like to see my patients suffering either. But we've got medicine for that."

"We've got medicine, too. But ours just doesn't wear off. Now…no more stalling—your weirdest story."

"Well, there was this one guy who got shot in the neck."

"By whom?"

"Angry girlfriend."

She narrows her eyes. "And this is going to have a happily ever after, right?"

"By some standards," I say. "He lived."

"Go on," she says.

"So he got shot in the neck, which normally would be, well, not a happy ending."

"I can imagine."

"But for this guy, the bullet sort of went through the front part of his neck and then lodged between his throat and the skin, so there was just this lump there. He could even talk. And we couldn't do anything about it, because if the bullet moved, it could be bad—like, if it was blocking a broken artery or something and it moved, he would bleed out. So we just helped him really slowly and talked him through it, and got him into the ambulance."

"And?" she asks.

"He survived," I say.

"The girlfriend?" she asks.

"No idea," I reply. "That's not my lane."

She presses her lips together. "Hopefully they broke up."

"Hopefully," I reply, "but the truth is that a shocking number of these couples stay together."

"Hmmm. What a job. To see people in some of their lowest moments, to treat them, and then to have no idea what happens after."

"Yeah," I answer. "It's both the best and worst thing about my job."

My steak arrives, her shrimp. I catch the waiter giving her a once over, but she doesn't seem to notice.

"And your mom's an engineer."

"Was," I correct.

"And your dad a lawyer. How did they feel about your job choice?"

"Mom was really supportive. She thinks it suits me."

"And your dad?"

"He wants me to become a lawyer."

"Of course," she answers, popping a piece of broccoli into her mouth. "Have you told him that's a little cliché?"

"I haven't talked to him in person for ten years."

"Oh, well, then I guess he doesn't get to have much of an opinion, does he?"

"Oh, he's got an opinion," I answer.

She sets her fork down, looks into my face. Suddenly the loud restaurant feels really quiet. "And do you feel like you should take it, his advice?" she asks.

"Sometimes," I answer.

She nods, looking away almost as though she's thinking about something else, then asks, "Why?"

"Because he still deposits money for it every six months."

She shakes her head. "Okay, plot twist. I wasn't expecting that answer. So he deposits money in your actual bank account?"

And for a minute I panic, feeling like a little kid. This woman has seen me hanging out with my mom on Sunday and now I've just told her my daddy still sends me money twice a year. "It's even worse than depositing it into an account," I say. "He gives it to my mom."

She wipes her lips with a napkin and underneath I can't tell if she's smiling or frowning. Maybe the date is over. Victoria would have lost it well before this point.

"I don't spend it," I say.

"What do you do with it?" she asks, putting the napkin down.

"Put it in a savings account. If I ever decide to do law, I'll use it. Otherwise, maybe I'll send it back to him one day."

She pushes her lips together. "But that's your interaction with him? Like, your only interaction? Just getting money."

"Not so cliché now, huh?" I ask, laughing. "He's always pressuring me to go back to school. He'll also call about once a year, usually on my birthday, and give his sales pitch."

"Which is?"

"Money, of course. It's always money."

"Isn't it though," she murmurs. She's mashing her potatoes into a flat pile, like she's thinking.

I cut a hunk of steak. "And he's not wrong. Sometimes—like when I get a new dog who has some unexpected medical bills—I wonder if maybe he's right and I should take his advice."

"And why is that?"

"Because it's solid advice. I *would* make more money."

"This is exactly how my sister feels about me becoming a veterinarian. Or maybe her personal assistant."

"No pressure from Dad, huh?"

She laughs. "My dad's an accountant and consultant who always has a busy season when he doesn't want to come to dinner."

"Seems reasonable enough," I reply.

"Like the rest of us don't know when the actual busy season is."

"Why don't you try that?" I ask. "Accounting."

"I'd kind of rather die. I do like numbers, but not other people's tax problems."

"Yeah, that sounds a little..." I pause. "A lot better than people's legal problems, actually, but still not fun."

"So basically the question is, what problems of other people would we like to help solving?" she says.

It's the perfect question, and one I never could have put into words.

She spears a shrimp, examines it. "If you did do law, what kind would it be?"

"I don't know," I say, "Accident, I guess, since that's where my area of expertise is. I've thought about it a little, and the truth is that if I'm going to go back to school, I guess I'd rather go into medicine. Maybe become a doctor. Trouble is, I didn't love school. I mean, it was fine, but becoming a doctor would mean a lot of school. Especially when I don't even know…"

"Yeah, I don't know what I want to do either," she says, cutting me off.

I pinch my lips together.

"What?" she says.

"What do you mean, 'what?'" I ask.

"You made a face."

"I didn't."

"You did. A face that said something I said was wrong."

I chew another piece of meat before answering her. "I *do* know what I want to do," I finally say. "This. My job, that I do, that I'm good at. It's just that my dad wants me to do something else."

"Yeah, the whole family expectations thing is always getting in my way too. You know, I wanted to go to school and just take a smattering of classes to see what I liked. But my sister said it was a horrible waste of time and money. She actually sat down with me and made me figure out what a fifth year of college would cost."

"How much?" he asks.

"A lot. And that's just for a basic community college."

"Money," I say. "Always interfering. If I made a jillion bucks doing what I do, no one would want anything else for me, but as it is—public servant and all—" I smile and she catches it.

"I know it's rude to ask," she says, "but how much?"

"About fifty grand a year," I answer. "Plenty for me, but not much if I have a family."

"Families chip in," she says.

I nod noncommittally. My family hadn't been functional enough to chip in, so it's hard to picture what it would look like if I ever got married. Mom had worked hard on her own, stashing money away for my future. While Dad had sent money conditional on the career that I chose.

Maybe if Dad had just been entirely out of the picture—a deadbeat or one-night stand—I wouldn't have resented his lack of financial support. But all those years, he just let Mom work her tail off, and now Mom has bills for her hospital stay and the rehab facility, and she's footing those alone too.

I'd offered to help once, and she'd actually laughed. "Oh, honey," she'd said. "I've got this. You just be you."

Which had made me feel kind of terrible.

"I have to admit," I say to Becca, "that sometimes it would be nice to have a bunch of money to dump on some of the problems that come up." It's something I'd never confessed to anyone before.

"Well, you've got more money to dump than I do," she says.

"Not a competition," I reply, not asking what her wage is.

She tells me anyway. "Half as much as you. Imagine that minus the cost of an extra year of classes. It'd be stupid."

"Doesn't sound stupid to me."

"I could work for my sister for three times as much as I make. The offer is right there on the table. Video editing. I'm decent at it, and she needs it done."

"And…?" I ask.

"I hate it."

I nod, and before I'm quite sure what I'm doing, I reach over and take her hand, wrapping two fingers around her forefinger. "Take the smattering of classes," I say. "Next semester. I dare you."

I feel the heat of her fingers, the soft squeeze she gives me back. "I never could resist a dare."

"I had a feeling," I say, leaning forward just as the waiter—check in hand—arrives at the table.

Becca leans back, our hands breaking apart.

"You're on."

Just then a familiar scent wafts by. "Thought you were fast," Victoria says, picking the check up off the table with two slender fingers—like it's a cigarette. "I've got the bill tonight," she says to the waiter.

"No," I interject. "You don't."

"Of course I do. It's my gift to you two kids."

"Victoria," I say.

"Already a new girl. That's more speed than I thought you had."

I glance at Becca, feeling the hot anger flow into my face.

"None of my business," Becca says, holding up her hands.

"But I'm still faster," she says, slipping a hundred dollar bill into the waiter's hand. "There, it's done. Get yourself a drink with the change."

And she's gone, into the busy crowd of the restaurant.

The waiter is still standing there, the money dangling in his hand.

And then Becca kind of snorts a laugh and holds up her hand for a high five. "Free food," she says. "Didn't know I was that cheap of a date."

I smile too, but I still feel the boil under my skin. "Listen, I'm so sorry."

"Don't worry about it," she says. "That was the most exciting thing that's happened to me on a date since my friend Macie fell in love with my date. But that's a story for another day."

"That it is," I say. "And I'm really sorry about Victoria. We went out a couple times, but that was a total jerk move."

"It was a power move. That's how she rolls."

"How do you know?" I ask. "Were you guys friends?"

She laughs. "We were colleagues. I worked for a few months at PetStop before finding Dr. Reynolds."

"And?" I ask.

"And it wasn't my absolute favorite job."

I nod.

She looks up at the waiter. "Bring us the change for that, please."

And I can see that he's a little bummed he won't

be keeping all the change from it. And I kind of admire Becca's own little power move.

"Do you *want* a post dinner drink?" she asks.

I glance at the drinks menu. A bunch of fancy beers, which feels a little like an oxymoron, an equal number of cocktails with goofy names, and a few basic wines. "Truth is, I wouldn't really know where to start."

"Me either," she says. "I have to choke down the toast at Thanksgiving."

"But there's an ice cream shop down the street," I say.

"Now you're speaking my language."

CHAPTER 18

LANCE

nd we do speak the same language.

"Okay," I say, as we walk back to our cars, ice cream cones in hand. The street has emptied out, and the only places left open are the restaurants and bars. "Favorite job? You said you'd had a bunch."

"The clinic," she answers, without even having to think about it.

"Really?" I ask, "but you still don't want to be a vet?"

"No," she answers. "I just...I want to get out of the animal field. I'm not sure you could understand this since your family is so different than mine, but it's all about animals, and I just...I guess I want out of the animal biz."

I smile, licking the melting cream off my cone. "You make it sound like it's the mafia or something." I pause. "It's not the mafia, right?"

"Only if the mafia deals in dogs, kittens, some backyard poultry, and one orphaned parakeet."

"Hmmm," I say. "Sounds like the mafia to me."

"Oh, also YouTube," she says.

"Yeah, it's getting more suspicious with every word. But you know what we haven't done?" I ask, bending my eyebrows together in the most sinister way possible.

She looks sideways at me.

"*Watched* your sister's YouTube channel."

"No," she says.

"Yes," I answer. "It'd be the perfect way to end the night."

"I'll never escape," she groans.

"Just one night," I coo.

"Fine, fine," she finally says. "My house or yours?"

"Let's head over to mine. Maverick is going to be lonely."

"Her foot!" Becca says suddenly. "I haven't had a look at it yet."

"Sounds like a plan then," I answer. "We kill two birds with one stone."

"Oh, Lance," she answers. "In my family we do not kill birds with stones. Or by any other means."

And boy is that the truth. Her sister's YouTube channel is filled to the brim with the most touching, sometimes cheesiest stories of animal rescue and companionship you could ever imagine.

Lost dogs found. Cats hit by cars rehabilitated by loving family members. I mean, have you ever seen a cat in a cast? Well, now I have. Disabled animals adopted. Birds rehomed after owners died. A horse that threw all its owners until a horse whisperer bought it for a song, and then lovingly tamed it. It's like every animal movie you've ever watched, but on steroids.

"I don't want to say, 'I told you so,'" she says. "But I totally told you so."

"You did," I answer.

"You and Maverick would have been a good story," she says.

I glance at her, scoot closer on the couch. "Would we?" I ask.

"Sure," she says. "Hurt puppy. Saved after a call, by a hot paramedic."

"Hot, huh?" I ask.

"I'm just saying that when emergency personnel start saving animals…well, EMS could probably get its own calendar after that."

I tip her face up, look into her eyes. "Maverick and I had a happy ending," I say.

She looks at me, the blue eyes dark in the dim room. "But the people you saved didn't."

"Do you want to hear it?" I ask. "You said only happily ever afters."

"I can hear it," she says.

"It was this couple. Their thirtieth wedding anniversary. They got hit by a semi at a cross section."

She looks down, bites her lip.

"I'm sorry," I say. "I don't have to tell you."

"No," she says. "You can. It must be hard to carry some of this stuff."

I don't answer. Truth is, my throat feels a little thick and I don't trust my voice. It *is* hard to carry some of this stuff. "The husband lived," I say. "The wife didn't."

She moves closer. "I'm sorry," she says. "I won't bring the story up again."

"No," I say. "It's okay, and I know you were just teasing. It's just…my job is a little different than your sister's channel, you know."

"I do," she says, now tipping my chin down to look into her face. "Or I'm starting to. Thanks for telling me, Lance."

"Thanks for hearing," I say. "Sometimes it just feels good to say the things to someone else."

And then her lips are on mine—soft and sweet and slow.

Slow.

Just how it should be. I lean down to her, one hand running through her hair, the other pressing against the small of her back.

We break away and I tip her forehead against mine, holding both her cheeks in my hands. She slips her arms around me and our lips meet again. Harder this time, but still so sweet. I put my arms fully around her, pull her in tight against my body. She wraps into it so perfectly.

And then I feel a small weight on my thigh. A little paw. Becca pulls away, smiles down at Maverick.

"Maverick," I say. "You weren't invited."

Maverick nudges closer, pushing between us.

"Awww," Becca says. "She's looking at me like I'm a home wrecker. But somehow it's the cutest thing."

It is kind of cute.

Becca glances at Maverick's foot. "It looks okay." She yawns, tenderly pressing on different places.

"You look tired," I say. "Let's examine Maverick's foot another time."

"Yeah," Becca says. "I probably *should* call it a night." She pats Maverick on the head, then draws Mavvy's ear through her fingers.

Now I'm the one who's jealous. I want her to draw my ear through her fingers just like that.

"I'll call you," I say.

"I'd be mad if you didn't," she answers.

She stands up and I scoop her into another kiss.

Maverick whines.

"You better get her outside," Becca says with a grin.

I give Maverick a mock scowl. "Seriously, girl?"

"Seriously," Becca says.

And then she's gone.

CHAPTER 19

LANCE

"Okay," Becca says, sitting in front of Maverick. She's got a bunch of papers strewn across the couch, and something else about ligaments pulled up on her phone. "It's obviously completely different than a human hand. The ligaments connect the joints of the toe. We have that too, but—you know—differently. Anyway, if one of them is hurt or torn or inflamed, she's going to have issues." She gently takes each of Maverick's toes, feeling along them.

Maverick sits patiently, letting her move along like it's doggy massage day. Until the third toe. Then Becca hits a point and Maverick lets out a whine. "Think we found it," she says.

I'm petting Maverick's back, trying to keep her calm.

"It's a little swollen," Becca says with a frown. "The question is whether it's from a pull or she's got something stuck in there from the accident. I'm sure Dr. Reynolds would have checked her whole foot, but what if something was lodged deep?"

She's moved to the next toe, and Maverick has settled back into doggie massage mode.

"So, let's say it's just a tear or something," I say. "There's really not much you can do, right?"

Becca moves back to the third toe and I rub Maverick by the ears to keep her calm. "I don't know. If she was a human, you'd ice it and rest it, and if it was bad—like completely torn or something—you'd get surgery. But she's been moving through life just fine."

She presses a little too hard and Maverick pulls her paw back.

"It does feel hard," Becca says. "Like something got trapped there. Of course, it could also be just some sort of bone spur or a corn or something. Reynolds could examine it further. But that's more money, and then what if it's nothing, or nothing anyone can do much about?" She pauses, her entire face pulled down in a frown. "I'm sorry, Lance. I thought I might be able to figure it out, but I just don't know."

I move from the floor to the couch, sitting beside both her and Maverick. I hold out a hand and Maverick puts her paw into it. "Good girl," I murmur. "If something is there and we could get it out, I'd want to. But wouldn't there be an infection if something was trapped there? There's no pus or anything."

"Not necessarily," Becca said. "Depending on the metal, it might just be like a piercing or something, only where it would cause pain when you stepped on it. Or the body could be containing the infection like it would with a wart. At least I think so—remember I'm not a trained professional."

I nod.

"I'm sorry I couldn't figure it out," she says, and it looks almost like she wants to cry.

"Hey," I say. "You're giving me a free consultation and trying to figure out an animal body when you're studying human bodies. It's okay. I'll take her back to Dr. Reynolds for an X-ray."

Becca still looks kind of miserable. "It makes me feel like I'm failing on all fronts. Family-animal-lover-and-rehabilitator plus studier-of-the-body-and-ligaments."

"You're not failing," I say, looking around at the clutter of papers. "Look, why don't you study while I make some dinner."

"You cook?" she asks.

"I'm a thirty-one-year-old bachelor," I answer. "I've got to have *some* skills."

She smiles, and it's so nice to see that I swear I'd make her dinner every night while she studied. "Any preferences? I've got chicken, sausage, peppers."

"Anything you like is good with me."

"Well, maybe I'll throw it all together," I say.

She lifts an eyebrow. She has the best eyebrow lift of anyone I've ever known.

"Trust me," I say. "It's going to be delicious."

*A*nd it is. Sausage and chicken first, then the onions and peppers to cook in the grease of the sausage, plus a dash of olive oil. Salt. It would have been fantastic just like that, but I add in a half cube of cream cheese and a can of diced tomatoes.

"It's divine," she says. "Don't tell my mom, but it might be better than her Sunday dinners."

"I will never tell. You can wrap it in a tortilla if you'd like, or put it over rice. I think I have some leftover in my fridge."

"It's perfect as is," she says, wolfing it down.

"Maybe tomorrow we can do it again," I say.

"I study and you make me food?" she asks. "It seems unfair."

"You're helping Maverick with her foot."

She snorts. "No I'm not."

"You are," I say. "Now I know she might need an X-ray."

"She might not," Becca counters. "She might just have a doggie corn. In fact, let me ask Reynolds first, before you spend more money."

"See," I say. "I'm getting all this free help. Plus, I get to have some company for dinner. Company who can talk," I say, glancing at Maverick, who is happily munching on the bits of chicken tendon that I cut off and gave her. "Maybe we can go for a w-a-l-k after dinner."

"I'd like that," Becca says.

"Unless it's bad for Mavvy," I add.

"If it's just a pull or tear, it's not bad; a little movement is good," she says. "A corn or bone spur, or maybe even just a malformation from birth—that's okay too. If it's a shard, then I don't know."

"We'll keep it short. Then you can study some more."

"Here?" she asks.

"Sure," I say. "Why not?"

She looks at me suspiciously, like I'm going to try to make out with her instead of let her study. I try to look as innocent as possible. I can't promise I won't steal a kiss or two, but if I have a choice of empty couch with just me and Maverick, or beautiful woman studying her heart out on said couch, I'm going to go with the second option. Even if we don't make out.

BECCA

I haven't talked to Sally Mae for a couple weeks. I called Mom to tell her I wouldn't be at dinner because…excuses. I threw myself into work and school. I messaged her the email address for one of the pet parents who said she was a huge fan of Sally's channel and had a cool story, but I didn't include any other text. She emailed me back with a quick 'thank you.' So, I mean, we could be doing worse as sisters. But we could definitely be doing better. I wonder if she's hired anyone yet for the editing.

I type a quick text, then decide that the girl power thing to do would be to call. Then I remind myself that she hasn't called me, and she's the older one. Then I remind myself…girl power, and click the button by her name.

It rings six times and I'm deciding if I should leave a voicemail or not when I hear her voice. "Hey Becca."

"Hey Sal."

A pause, nice and awkward. "It's been a couple of weeks. I was studying last Sunday for this big exam."

"Good," she says. "How's school going?"

"It's good," I answer, my voice tipping up just a bit. "Really interesting stuff." I almost tell her about the ligament research thing, but I stop. She isn't asking for more details. And what would I tell her if she did? Small talk about ligaments and tendons isn't exactly small talk at all. It's nerd talk.

"Did you hire an editor yet?" I ask.

She doesn't answer immediately, then finally says, "Allen has been helping me in the evenings."

Up goes the guilt.

"Honestly," she goes on, and I have to shove off the guilt just to hear what she's saying. "I did hire someone. For about a week. She was awful. So then I fired her."

"Shoot," I say, the guilt making another appearance in my gut. "I'm sorry. That sounds really stressful."

She laughs. "You know, it kind of was. I've never had to fire someone before."

I cut back a comment about that being because she didn't pay me for half the stuff I did. I'm glad I do, because the next thing out of her mouth is pretty darn near to an apology.

"I didn't realize what a good job you did with it."

"Oh," I say.

"Surprised to hear me say it?" she asks with another laugh.

"Well...yes," I answer. And suddenly I see my sister as more than a domineering girl boss, but as a woman with a family and a job who was trying to do something really good in the world. Something that isn't easy, that most people don't do. "And thank you," I add.

"You're welcome," she replies. "You keeping the grades up?" Ah, there's the bossy back again.

"I am," I answer. "Now you're the one who's surprised to hear it, right?"

"Naw," Sally Mae answers. "I knew you'd shine when you cared enough."

"Sally," I begin, pushing away any lingering guilt, so I can say what I'm going to say without it. "I've got a few hours on Saturday morning to help you out. And I can make some other time during the week too."

"You don't have to," she answers.

"I know," I say. "I know I don't. And I really don't want to forever, but maybe I can help here or there while you find someone who's really qualified for the job."

"Allen has it under control."

"With his day job and your two kids?" I ask. "Three hours. Send me that much work this week and I'll get it back to you by Sunday morning."

"You sure?" she asks.

"Yes," I answer. And I really am. I think it's the first time that I've been allowed to do something for Sally, not because she assumed it would be done, but because I really wanted to.

I'm about to burst with joy when I get to Lance's condo.

I knock twice, then let myself in, and am surprised to see Macie sitting on his couch. I do a double take. For a weird moment, I feel like maybe my brain went into some strange autopilot and took me to the wrong house. Then Macie starts to laugh. "Becca, the look on your face."

"Listen," I say, glancing around, still a little confused, but laughing at Macie's laugh anyway. "I already lost one potential boyfriend to you. You can't have another."

"From the looks of things, it's more than *potential* boyfriend territory at this point."

"What makes you say that?" I ask, sitting down across from her. Maverick trots over to me instantly and puts her head on my lap.

Macie just smirks. "Exhibit A. The guard dog— she seems to, uh, know you."

Just then, Lance walks in with a glass of water for Macie. "Becca!" he says, like he too is having a little trippy confusion. He looks back and forth between us. "Do you guys know each other?"

"Best friends," I answer.

"I'm the matronly one, in case you were wondering," Macie says with her perfect deadpan.

Lance laughs. "You want a water, Becca?"

"Sure," I say. "But maybe also to know why my girl Macie is sitting on your couch."

"She had a question about a call," Lance answers.

"Unofficial of course," Macie says.

"Of course," I say. "Where's Tad?" I ask.

"Talking to the other medic," she answers. "We wanted the stories separately."

"Is Lance in trouble?" I ask, only mostly joking. "You're not going to arrest him or something, are you?"

"Not unless he robbed the house where his last call was. Did you?" she asks. "I could have Becca cuff you."

"Maybe later," Lance says with his own impressive deadpan. "Though I think I'd rather be eternally poor than touch anything in that hoarder house."

"What do you mean?" I ask, settling into the couch. Maverick jumps up beside me.

"The guy was a hoarder," Lance says. "When we got there, he was on his bed—chest pain. But this house, Becca. You can't even imagine it. Stuff everywhere. Papers, cans, bottles, clothes. There wasn't even a path through the garbage. He's just lying there on his bed and the stuff is piled almost as high as the top of the bed."

"Really?" I say.

"Really," he answers. "And there wasn't a clearing through the stuff. I just walked over it—clothes and packages of food that were surely expired, empty, dirty cans and bottles."

Macie clucks. "Turns out some hoarders hoard a

lot of money," she says. "And someone must have known. Tad and I are trying to figure out if it looked different on that call before they took the patient to the hospital than it looked afterwards."

"Did it?" I ask, leaning in. "This is way, way more exciting than the cat who came to the clinic today with ringworm."

"It's hard to say," Lance replies, though Macie looks like she would have known if she'd been on that call. "Like I say, it was just a gross disaster. I didn't want to touch anything. But I had to walk over it."

Macie's closing her eyes, like she's picturing something. "Do you think you would have bent or broken things?" she asks. "When you walked over it?"

"Yeah, I imagine," he answers. "The guy had a bunch of cans. Used tin cans. Like he hoped to one day recycle them and earn his fortune."

"He didn't need to earn a fortune," Macie says. "He already had one. But that does help."

"How?" Lance asks.

"Because there was no clear path of bent cans. In fact the cans had been moved around the room—the bent ones. Still on top of the rubbish, but strategically scattered. That means our guy's money was taken after you arrived, after he went to the hospital."

"Can this day get any cooler?" I murmur. "How is your job so cool?"

"I literally had to climb over ten years of a man's garbage. It wasn't that cool," Lance says, plopping down on the other side of Maverick. "And there were roaches."

"Did he live?" I ask.

"Apparently long enough to figure out he'd been robbed," he answers. "Of about ten thousand dollars."

I whistle, then glance between Lance and Macie. "Wait. How did you know to come ask Lance about all this?"

"Our detective called the station, found out who the medic on the call was."

"But you said it was unofficial?" I reply.

Macie smiles. "I recognized Lance's full name when they gave it to me. Much more helpful than you, Becca."

"What do you mean you recognized it?"

Lance smooths Maverick's ears. "I used to go the dentist Macie worked for."

A little look of sadness crosses over Macie's face.

"Rachel?" I ask.

Lance nods. "I was actually with Aiden on the call where he broke his tooth. I was the one who told him I had a great dentist."

"Really?" Macie says, leaning forward, like she's listening to her grandmother tell a story about some bygone thing.

"Really," Lance says. "And he listened."

"You were at their wedding," Macie says, studying his face. "I just didn't make the connection."

"Yes," he says. "And the funeral."

"I wasn't looking around that day," Macie says. "I couldn't have found a single face in that crowd, except Aiden and Gabby."

"I think a lot of us felt that way," Lance says. "It was awful."

"It was."

"You know, sometimes I feel a little guilty for getting them together. I didn't want them to hurt."

"They didn't," Macie says. "I mean, they did hurt, but not because they were together. That was the only thing that made the whole disaster bearable. So, never regret it. If we could all live and die with that much love around us, the world would be a perfect place."

Macie's eyes have gone glassy and when I look at Lance, I notice that his have too. Maverick reaches up and licks his hand, like she knows. I reach over to his other hand, and smile at Macie.

She clears her throat. "Well, that's a long way off from theft. Tad never would have let the conversation go that far off topic. Back to hoarders."

"It's hard to get away from them sometimes, to be honest," Lance says with a laugh.

"Did they find the money?" I ask.

"No," Macie answers.

"Then how do you know it even existed? What if it's just a delusion?"

"A possibility," Macie replies. "But he had another stash, also substantial."

"You're kidding," I say.

"I'm not," she replies.

"Do they have any leads about who took it?" Lance asks.

"Well, the victim has several neighbors he hates, but none of them knew about it. Which leaves a few relatives, plus several random women from bars."

"Or this guy," I say, stabbing my thumb in Lance's direction.

He throws up his hands in mock surrender, and Maverick looks offended by the suddenness of the gesture. "Hey, I didn't know about it either. And wouldn't have believed it if I had."

"Which brings us to the real question, the crucial question," Macie says, closing her eyes again. "Who would?"

Lance looks at her like he's impressed. I know how he feels. Even Maverick is gazing at her. "Good luck," Lance says. "I hope you crack the case."

"Me too," she replies. "When you have a second, would you text me a sketch of the room the way you remember it?"

He shrugs. "I'm not much of an artist, but if you don't mind stick figures and symbols."

"That'll work," she says, standing and stretching.

"And I can't imagine much has changed with all that trash piled around."

"I can't either," Macie says. "Which is why I want to know if anything has. Try to remember as much as you can, even if it seems dumb."

"I'll do my best," Lance says doubtfully, "but I get a little hyper focused on calls. All I cared about was figuring out if the patient was having a heart attack or not. The only reason I even noticed the trash was because I had to step on it."

"Your best is fine," Macie says. "Now you guys better get on with your night." She gives me a pointed look.

"Well," Lance says when she's gone. "I guess we've both got homework tonight."

He doesn't seem very excited about his.

"We'll take breaks," I say coyly, leaning over and giving him a kiss.

"Yeah," he says, pulling me close. "We'll need to. Breaks are good for your brain."

"The best," I add.

We only kiss for a minute before I tip away. "I almost forgot my news!" I say. "It's not quite as wild as going to a hoarder house for a guy with a heart attack and then getting a visit from an unofficial detective, but…"

"What?" he asks, his voice going up with interest.

"Well, okay, I hope I didn't overbill it, but…drum roll please…Sally apologized to me."

"That's great," he says, pulling me in. "You know, forget homework. We should relax tonight. Celebrate. Maybe buy a pizza. Watch a movie together."

"That would be so fun," I say. "But I really can't. I've got this big test coming up and the research for my professor is due soon. Plus, I need to be in bed early tonight because of work. And because I told Sally I'd help a bit till she finds a replacement."

Lance kind of narrows his eyes. "Is she going to find someone?"

"You know," I say. "I really think she is."

He looks tired.

"We can always celebrate like this," I say, reaching up for a kiss.

"That's better than pizza," he answers.

But even after the kiss, he still seems tired.

"I'll buy us some dinner," I say. "Have it delivered."

"No, it's good. You're busy. I'll make us something."

CHAPTER 21

LANCE

’ve put the sketch off as long as possible. I'm really not artistically inclined. But it'd be a jerk move to not do it at all. And it's been three days.

I pencil the layout of the house, as best as I can remember. Then get distracted, thinking of the man's heart rhythm—the only thing I'd been truly concerned about at the time. I sketch that out too, though I know it's not what Macie wants.

With my pencil, I follow the mountains and valleys of the heart, thinking about Becca.

I haven't dated anyone this seriously, well, ever. But she's so busy, and sometimes things feel off. She's spent the last three days working, home-working (not with me), and extra working for Sally.

She promised she'd be here tonight, but it's already after seven, and she's not.

I draw the hoarder's bed in the corner—pushed tight against the wall. Probably so he could make as much room as possible for the other stuff.

Old boxes, from everything—cereal, packages, tissues. Cans that had been rinsed and saved, though they still stank with the remnants of food. That two-inch roach that had climbed over my boot. Probably not what Macie is wanting a sketch of. Tons of papers—in stacks and clips. Magazines, old newspapers. Bottles from Cokes and beers and pasta sauce.

Truthfully, I'd be surprised if there wasn't a fortune's worth of recycling in that house after all. Or change buried beneath the mountains of stuff.

I glance at Becca's spot on the couch. Empty. Maverick seems disappointed about it too, and has positioned her head right where Becca's lap would be.

A couch, I think suddenly. There was one in the room somewhere too. It was almost completely buried, but when I first came in, I'd banged my shin on it, and realized what it was.

In my mind, it seems like it must have been along the wall by the door. Yes, since I banged my shin just after we'd come in. Or had it been in the center of the room? I close my eyes like Macie did. Nope. Nothing.

All I see is my jump kit, feel its weight, the crunch of my boots as I walked over things. Some parts squishy with clothes and paper, some hard with bottles and full boxes. And, yes, the bend of the cans.

I draw my path. I do remember that part, remember it perfectly. The door on the southeast side of the room. It was open about a foot and a half and we had to shove it open a little more to try to get our equipment in.

We ended up leaving the cot in the hall and just bringing in the backboard. Jordan was carrying the back end. I had a hand on the front end, and the strap for the jump kit slung over my shoulder. A straight diagonal to the bed.

I like straight lines, clear-cut calls.

I think again of Becca, wonder if our line is straight. I'd thought it was. It had seemed really clear and simple. But now it feels like it's starting to squiggle.

I glance back at my sketch. I've pressed my pencil hard along that straight line. It's dark and clear. When I got to the patient, I'd hooked up him to the

EKG, checked the heart rhythm, then rolled him—moaning—onto the backboard.

My partner and I had dragged him back over the rubble, through the door that we had to force open even more. I sketch a wiggly line to show the shift of the door—we got it open about six extra inches and it was hard. Squeezed through. Then backboard to cot to ambulance. The hallways were clear-ish at least.

And that's all I've got for Macie.

I wonder if she's got advice for me. It's not that I want to pull Becca away from her studies or family or work or anything.

It's just that I want to pull her to me, and some-times it feels like all those other things come first—all of them. And sometimes it feels like they always will. Am I okay with that?

It's probably not the type of question Macie can answer—no matter how good of a detective she is, no matter how hyper observant.

I take a quick picture of the sketch, and email it to Macie.

So now *my* homework's done. But the only company I've got is Maverick.

Becca was supposed to come over last night, and

cancelled. Research due, and she wanted it to look perfect.

Tonight she promised she'd come as soon as she was done with the edits for Sally. Question is, how long will that take?

I make a sandwich for myself, give Maverick the final bit. "Guess we're walking alone tonight, girl," I say.

Maverick wags her tail on the word 'walk.' Though she does look around the empty room before we leave.

I realize that I do too.

***

Becca shows up just after nine. I'm watching a movie and thinking about going to bed early.

She squeezes between me and Maverick on the couch.

"Tired?" I ask.

"Yeah," she says. "But I took my midterm today and got the edits for Sally done. I'm all yours."

"I'm glad to get you back," I say, kissing her head.

She nuzzles against me and falls asleep almost instantly. I settle in, enjoying the warmth of her.

I don't wake her until the movie's over. "Do you want me to drive you home?" I ask.

"No, that'd be silly," she says. "How would I get my car in the morning?"

"But you're so tired," I say.

"Nah, I'm good. Just needed a little catnap." She stretches.

"Do you want to stay?" I ask.

She pops that perfect eyebrow.

"Just for sleep," I say. "You're so tired."

"Nah, it's okay," she says. "I need my toothbrush and pajamas."

"Okay," I say, walking her to the door. She leans in for a sleepy kiss. And I hold her there for as long as I can.

"Work," she finally says.

And I know it's late, so I let her go.

CHAPTER 22

BECCA

I arrive home, tired, but happy. Midterm done. Research turned in. Sally's edits done. And, finally, a low-key night with Lance. Even if I did sleep most of it away. Hopefully that wasn't too obnoxious.

If Sally's found an editor, the second half of the semester should be a lot easier, and if I nailed my midterm like I think I did…

I glance at my laptop. I need to get to bed, but my midterm should be graded and showing up by now, and it will only take a second.

I feel a little swoop of nervousness as I log in. Which is silly, considering I studied so hard for Bio, and I loved every minute of it. Maybe not quite as much as I loved anatomy, but still a lot. And I got Bio —my brain just understood. Plus, I loved how I could apply it to the anatomy class. It all fit together, and it's starting to feel like maybe my life will too.

Which is why it takes me several seconds to process the fat C- that stares at me from my screen. But, how? Had I gotten offline with the multiple choice questions and filled in the wrong bubbles; had I been confused about one of the basic functions of cells? Who knows? Tomorrow I'll get the actual paper back, the actual paper with the red X's, with that score, 70—almost a D, at the top of the paper.

Tonight I close out my computer. The lights are dim. Through that light, I stare at the door. From it, I imagine several voices. My sister telling me how much money I could make from editing her videos— a position that, as far as I know, is still available. My mom expecting me to follow in Sally's footsteps. And, last but never least, Lance's look the other night when I needed to study. His face kind of pulling down like he was so tired. But not from work. No. It was from me, from this, all of it. When he signed up for a girlfriend, not two college classes.

I take off my shoes, slip out of my clothes. Normally, I read the next day's chapter, write out the terms, study anything that seems confusing. Tonight, I close the book, drop my notebook into my backpack. Then stare at it for a moment. A backpack. Aren't I a little old for that, a little old for this whole stupid thing?

I still brush my teeth (if the test had asked about *streptococcus mutans* or *porphyromonas gingivalis*, I could have answered that). I don't bother with pajamas and sink into my bed. I can't say I'm asleep in minutes, no matter how numb I feel.

I leave the backpack at home when I go to work the next day. Normally, I work, then head to class, then make my way to Lance's house for some food, a walk with Maverick, and more studying. Just thinking about it makes me cringe a little. I must be the worst girlfriend in the history of ever—expecting food, then going for a walk, then working on my school stuff.

By the time my class rolls around, I'm feeling antsy. I slump into my seat and the professor passes the papers back just like it's high school. High school again. Is that the life I've chosen? And just like high school, I flip my test over really briefly, feel the rush of heat in my cheeks, and flip it back. He's going over the midterm now, but I'm having trouble focusing. It all sounds like stuff I knew—know. Why would I have missed the questions on the test? Maybe it was the essays at the end. Maybe I should have put an English class on my roster so I could turn in a few decent paragraphs.

And then it's on to the next section—information I normally would have read about the night before. Without that, I definitely find it harder to follow the lecture.

I can't get away fast enough.

I hope Lance has made some kind of comfort food, or maybe we can just eat cake. In fact, I swing by the grocery store on the way there and pick up the chocolate-y-est one I can find, and a quart of ice cream. Maybe that'll dull the pain.

When he opens the door, I want to collapse into his arms, tell him all about it—the blown test, not knowing why. I want to ask, "Is this a waste of my life? What am I even doing?"

But instead I give him my brightest smile, and hold out the cake.

"Celebrating, huh?" he asks with a big smile. "That midterm must have gone well."

I try to smile, make some sort of joke, but then Maverick nuzzles her soft snout into my hand and I feel the ears brush my leg and I know she knows.

My face feels like it cracks open. "Maybe not super well," I reply.

Lance sees it—that look of alarm on his face as the tears pour out and I can't stop them. "Hey," he says. "It's okay. Not all tests go perfectly."

I can't even speak and Maverick is making circles around me, pressing and nudging like she's trying to make it all better. I squat down and bury my face in her fur.

"Did you fail?" Lance asks. "Maybe they graded it wrong somehow."

I shake my head.

"Do you want to go over it?" he asks. "I'd ask if you want me to help, but unless it's about emergency medical stuff, I'd be pretty useless."

"Maybe less useless than me," I say. Then, "You should put the ice cream in the freezer before it melts."

He smiles, sitting next to me on the floor. "So...it was for grief, not celebration?"

I try to smile back. "Yeah, I guess."

"It's okay to fail a test," he says. "It happens to the

best of us. You should have seen some of the work I did in my lit class."

"I didn't really fail it," I say finally.

Maverick has settled into my lap, almost like a toddler, and I'm rubbing her ears through my fingers.

"You didn't fail?" he says.

"No," I respond. "C- though. It felt like a fail after all that work."

And then Lance actually laughs. And maybe it should make me laugh too—silly little me and all. But it doesn't.

"C- isn't the worst grade in the world," he says. "Again, you should have seen some of my papers for lit."

"I've spent all this time on it, studying, writing notes, listening to podcasts even. I should have nailed it. I *thought* I'd nailed it. Why did I feel so good about it and then do so bad?"

"You didn't do so bad," he says again. "You did average."

"Average minus," I say in a miserable voice, that—again—makes Lance laugh, but not me.

"Ah, Becca," he says, pulling me close. "It's really okay. Let's take the night off, do something fun."

"Okay," I say, feeling kind of miserable at the

prospect. "But first I should put on my big girl panties and have a look at the test."

"You haven't looked at it yet?" he asks.

"Nope," I say.

"Well, then, don't," he replies. "Not tonight. After all, we've done a lot of getting to know Biology. Let's spend tonight getting to know just us."

I've got my hand on the test in my purse, the test I couldn't look at. I realize that I brought it here so that I could get some emotional support in looking at it. That it was my plan—to get here, look at it, go over it, figure things out, and start again with the studying.

And I realize in a rush that that's not at all what Lance wants.

He wants me to ignore the test. He thinks it's silly to worry about a C-, though it might drag my whole grade down. He wants to have more 'us time'—time to get to know each other.

Get to know each other.

So I shove the test into the bottom of my purse, put class and science—those things that lit me up—out of my head as much as I can.

"Sure, we can go out," I say. It's what you say when you're cute, what you say when you're agreeable, what you say when your perfectly sweet boyfriend just wants a little "us" time.

And why not? Maybe that test was a sign, a sign that it's time for a course correction. So, yes, why (when you're thirty-one years old and you're not even succeeding at the community college bio), why not go have some fun with your boyfriend?

CHAPTER 23

LANCE

Wednesday night Becca shows up at my door.

"Hey," I say. "What are you doing here?"

"Bringing you a pizza," she replies.

"That's cool." I kiss her on the forehead. "Did your class get cancelled?"

"Cutting," she says.

I frown, carrying the box of pizza into my kitchen and pulling out a few plates. "That's not like you."

"It is tonight," she says. This time she's the one pulling me in for a kiss. It's sweet and long and melty. I press into it.

"Hey, I'm sorry," she says. "You deserved more of

my time, more of me. After all, you weren't the one who signed up for that class."

That night I get her time.

After the pizza, I'm in the mood for root beer floats, so we drive to the store together to buy soda and ice cream.

"You didn't buy caramel," she says, like I've committed a sin.

"I didn't realize that was part of the recipe."

"I'll just pretend I didn't hear that," she says, tossing a bottle in the cart. "I mean, my mom always makes it from scratch, so this is already a compromise."

"*We* could make it from scratch," I say.

She looks at me. "You know how?"

"No, but I have this thing called the internet."

"Caramel's tricky."

She's not wrong.

It takes us three batches and so much butter I wish we'd thrown more of that in the cart. But the end product is one of the best things I've ever eaten. "Tell your mother 'thank you,'" I say, as I eat yet another sample of the homemade caramel.

"And then just a little salt," Becca says, grinding a bit on top of the caramel.

Truly, it's the most divine root beer float one could imagine.

"You're amazing," I say.

"I didn't do anything but try to buy caramel."

"And I'm so glad you did." I lean back and pat my belly. "Now studying?"

"Are you kidding?" she says. "Now, a movie. Last time I fell asleep after about twelve seconds. And all for that stupid test."

I open my mouth to say that it wasn't stupid, then close it again.

"Favorite movie?" she asks. "Of all time. Let's watch that."

"I don't know," I say. "Maybe *Indiana Jones*."

"Done," she replies, picking up the remote and settling onto the couch. Maverick settles with her. It feels funny that I'm the last one. As soon as I sit, Becca scoots closer, leaning in for a kiss. A whole series of them, sweet and slow. Then Maverick wiggles closer to both of us, and we laugh.

It's almost 1:30 when the credits finally roll. Becca almost made it to the end before nodding off. Her head is nestled onto my shoulder and I wrap my arms around her, feeling the steady breaths. Maverick is also asleep—curled into that cat-like circle by Becca's hip.

I slip out from under Becca, easing her onto the couch, then covering her with a blanket. I lean over and kiss her forehead—softly enough that she won't wake up.

The next morning when she wakes up, I've got eggs, sausage, and peppers cooking.

"That smells amazing," she says. "But how are you up? Don't you sleep?"

"I'm used to weird hours."

She settles onto the bar stool, running her tongue over her teeth. "That was maybe not my best life choice. Next time I'm bringing a toothbrush."

I smile and lean over to kiss her.

"Mmm, do that again," she says.

I do. Again, and again. Until the sausage almost burns, and I have to run to it.

"Last night was fun," she says, "even though I do feel like I have a hangover."

"All we drank was a liter of root beer," I respond, flipping her egg.

"Maybe that'll do it," she answers.

I slip her an Ibuprofen with her breakfast. "I know you're usually a morning person."

"Yeah," she says, rubbing her head and gulping down the pills.

"But I really appreciated the time," I say.

She nods, her eyes still a little dazed. She takes a few bites of her breakfast, then gasps. "I've got to get to work. I was thinking it was a Saturday or something."

"See you this weekend," I reply, thinking it'll be a few days before she can come over again.

But that night she's back. This time with a bag of groceries. "Sorry I had to rush off during breakfast," she says.

"I mean, you had to go to work," I answer. "Don't you need to study tonight?"

She shrugs, plopping the groceries down on my counter—everything she needs to make carbonara. I watch as she makes the pasta, prepares the eggs and cheese, chops the garlic and a few hot peppers. Her hands fast, competent. She'd been surprised that I cooked, and now I'm surprised at her. "Where did you learn to make this?"

"My mom, of course," she says.

"It's perfect. Is your mom single?" I ask.

"Hardy har har," she says. "And no. You'll have to find someone else who makes perfect Italian." She bats her eyelashes.

"Yeah," I say. "I'll have to keep my eyes peeled for someone like that." I take a bite and close my eyes and it's the best thing I've ever tasted. "You should quit your job and do this for a living," I say, winding more pasta around my fork.

"Do you really think I should quit my job?" she asks.

"What? No. I just...this is really good." I expect her to leave afterwards, but she doesn't. We stay up talking and kissing until, again, she falls asleep on the couch. This time I scoot her into my bed, and then I take the couch. I wake her when I know she'll need to be up, and I have a quick breakfast waiting for her. "Becca," I say, as she rushes around. "That was really nice, but..."

She kisses me really quick and is gone.

The entire week goes like this and the first part of the next.

It should be perfect, everything I've ever wanted right there in a rush of time and love and commitment.

But something's missing.

It's hard to pinpoint what it is exactly. She's still laughing, but when she does, I feel like part of her isn't there. She's still talking, but she carefully avoids any conversation about classes or the subjects that I could barely get her to stop talking about before.

Now we discuss the movies we've watched or office gossip or my worst calls compared to her worst animals stories (it's hard to choose a winner). When she skips her Wednesday class for the second week in a row, I start to wonder what's really going on.

This time, when she falls asleep on the couch (she didn't even make it until midnight), I notice she's brought a leather purse. Maverick's going to smell that a mile away. But when I move it so Maverick doesn't eat it, an open notebook slips out.

It's then that I find what's missing.

At least four assignments for starters. I see them highlighted in her notebook, but nothing's been started. She also has a small pink slip from one of her professors with a warning that if she doesn't turn a paper in by next Monday, she'll risk failing the class.

I tuck the papers back into her bag.

The thing that was missing. It's her. The real her. The one who got excited about bones and ligaments. The one who wanted to break free of the expectations people had for her. Something that's hard to do when those people matter to you in your life—whether it's your sister, or your new boyfriend.

I try to remember our conversation before she skipped that first class and brought me a pizza. She was really upset about that grade, and I had kind of brushed it off.

I mean, truly, a C- is fine, but I didn't mean to tell her that it didn't matter—it clearly did to her. And what mattered to her mattered to me. I had seen the way she lit up about her classes, about science in general—it was beautiful—and I had wanted her to succeed because she wanted it.

But is that what I had communicated? Maybe not.

That night of that conversation something had shifted. And the next day, she'd said something, something that replays now in my head. *You deserve more of my time. After all, you weren't the one who signed up for that class.*

Well, maybe it was time that I did.

CHAPTER 24

BECCA

Friday night. Lance tells me he's got a surprise for me. Is it weird that I'm not excited to get it?

Truth be told, I haven't been excited about much of anything these last few weeks, including our dinners and evenings together. I don't even want to think about sex and I'm grateful Lance hasn't broached the subject.

I grab my keys, a light jacket.

Professor Davis has given me a warning, a warning that feels a lot like an ultimatum. If I want to pass Bio, then I'm going to have to get my paper in before Monday. It's generous of him to even give me that final warning, but what's the point? I haven't even started it.

Originally I meant to. I didn't mean to give Lance all my time. I was going to squeeze my studying into the morning hours or maybe the late ones. But that never happened. In fact, it's begun to look like it's going to be one or the other—a relationship or a passing grade.

And I'm definitely better at one than I am the other (insert knowing wink).

I sigh. A knowing wink isn't really what I wanted.

I open the car door and slump in.

I miss my classes, miss my detours online when I dove into studies about ligaments and bones and circulation. Mmmm, circulation—that'd be a cool research paper. And that's exactly the problem with me. I mean, who even feels that way?

Nobody. Not my mom for sure. Even Sally Mae, with her love of animals and biology. Even Lance with his medical background. He doesn't care about how different veins grow, how food and the environment might affect them. He only cares about stopping someone from bleeding out, or getting a dead heart to beat. And those seem like pretty valuable things. As opposed to recognizing the difference between male and female circulatory systems.

I tap the steering wheel. It's not *fun*, not normal fun anyway. It's just so…fascinating.

I set the thought aside. Setting things aside is a skill I've been working to master these last couple weeks.

Lance has given me an address and I'm supposed to meet him there.

When I pull up, it's easy to see where this is leading. It's a Best Western—a nice one. A romantic gesture, I guess. But it doesn't feel romantic to me at all.

I pull my jacket tighter over my body, wishing I'd opted for an oversized hoodie instead of the sleek red top I've got on. This just isn't the direction I wanted things to go, not right now.

I sit in my car, trying to push down the small rage that's rising when I get a text.

"Meet me at room 37. You can come around the back. I've propped the door open."

"I'd rather you just meet me at my car," I text back. He and I, we need to talk.

"Just trust me," he messages. "I've got a surprise for you."

Great. This is not the way I want to have this conversation.

"Lance, really…" I start typing the message.

"Just trust me."

I tip my head back, sighing. Make my way to the

back door, which is propped open with a rock from the parking lot. Nice. My bag is light without my textbooks. The fact that I think of that as I enter a hotel for a surprise from my boyfriend, well, it just seems like a bad sign.

Room 37 is also propped open, and honestly, it's good that I do trust him. Otherwise, I would be starting to wonder if I was about to be murdered.

The room is dark, but it smells nice; he's got several candles burning in different corners. It's all the light I have and as soon as I walk in, he shuts the door behind me.

I jump, maybe even let out a small squeal. He laughs and wraps me into a hug there in the dark. "Just me," he whispers into my ear. At least he still has all his clothes on; otherwise, this conversation would have been even more awkward.

My heart is hammering, and I open my mouth to begin, to get it over with, to say, *I can't do this. Not like this. Not now. I don't know why, but everything's off kilter*, when he flips on the lights.

I expect to see roses, maybe a bottle of wine or a pair of sexy underwear. I take in a breath to begin my speech, but can't get it out because there are no roses, no bathrobes. Just a desk with my textbooks, several fresh notebooks, and my laptop. Also a pot of black coffee.

"Your favorite creamer is in the fridge," he says, tapping on it.

He's grinning ear to ear, but I still haven't figured out what's going on. Are we supposed to share a romantic night together with my textbooks? It almost feels cruel—the things I gave up taunting me the whole time. "Lance, I…"

"I've got a pack of fresh pens. And I know you're not one to pull an all-nighter, so you can sleep and then wake up early if that's better for you."

Better for me?

I stare at him.

"It's for you," he says, seeing my confusion. "To study."

I open my mouth; nothing comes out.

"I knew I was getting in the way. I wanted to do something for you. This is it. A chamber of nerdiness right here for you."

I laugh then—a small sound, still a little confused, almost like a sniff. "So you, this, it's for me to study." And then, "With you?"

"Only if I can help. I was planning to hop out in an hour or so, so you can really get down."

I snort out a laugh. "Lance, this is so nice, but I'm still not sure I understand."

"I want to support you. I know you have stuff due, and your final is coming."

"It's going to take more than one night to clean up that mess," I grumble, so sad about it that I suddenly want to cry.

He must see it because he wraps me into a hug. "Then you can have more than one night."

I look up at him. "This is really nice," I say.

He nods, looking like he wants something else, so I reach up and kiss him.

"None of that," he says, laughing, but something's missing from it, and from this whole thing. "What's wrong?" he asks.

"Everything's perfect," I say, but only because I don't know what's wrong, don't know what feels so sick in my stomach. I don't have to have an awkward conversation about sex, don't have to explain my needs. He guessed them, then orchestrated a solution. Which, I realize in a rush, IS the problem.

"This is nice," I repeat, but there's a pause in my voice. We both hear it.

"And?" he says.

"It's sooo nice," I say. "But I think. Well, don't I need to be the one to make the decision?"

He cocks his head to the side, and looks a little like Maverick when he does.

"I mean," I try to explain—to him, and to myself, "it's still you making decisions for me."

He frowns, and I can see all the chivalry drain out of his face.

"And that's not a you problem," I say. "It's a me problem. I can't just keep doing this, letting everyone else figure me out, figure my needs out, make decisions for me."

I look around the room, at the cooling coffee, the fresh white notebooks. "I'm so sorry, but I think I just need a minute to figure myself out."

"And by a minute, you mean more than a minute." His voice has taken on a bit of a frost and the truth is that I want to shoot him that cute little smile of mine, throw him a kiss, and make it all go away, make it all not hurt right now. Which is just the problem—the me problem—and has been for a while.

It's not really that people see me as cute. Well, they do, but then I work to keep that place of, of… homeostasis. I glance at my biology book. "Yeah, more than a minute."

He shrugs, but it's a surprisingly sharp gesture. "Okay," he says. "The room is yours till 11:00

tomorrow. I guess you can do whatever you want with it."

"It was so nice," I repeat, but he's already got his back to me. One way or another, he's already gone.

When the room is completely quiet and it's just me and the books for the classes that I'm practically failing, and those blank, blank notebooks, I turn my back too. Curl up into a ball on the bed, and cry. A hard, ugly, lonely cry.

I don't know how long it lasts, or the sleep that follows, but when I wake up, clothes rumpled, the sun is just creeping in through the blinds. My eyes hurt, my teeth feel fuzzy, and I'm too thirsty for coffee.

In a small bag in the corner, I find a pair of pajamas, along with a fresh change of clothes and my toothbrush. I brush away the fuzz from my teeth, the bacteria, then rinse my face with cold water. I fill up one of the Styrofoam cups with water from the faucet, and run my fingers through the waves that are winding and tangling their way down my back.

The clock reads 6:00 am. Lance said I had until

eleven. My paper is due Monday. I pick up the remote, then put it down.

What, exactly, *do* I want? Not to watch the morning shows or cartoons. That much I know. Not to curl up on that bed again; I'm too awake. Not to go home where everything will wait for me like it was when I left it.

What do *I* want?

To nail that class, just like I always wanted. Just like I wanted when I first signed up. And while the ship might have sailed for acing it, it hasn't quite sailed for not failing it.

I plunk down at the desk and pour myself a cup of cold coffee, but I don't really need it. I slept well, and my mind feels clearer than it has in weeks. Turning to chapter one, I'm surprised by how much I remember, and even more surprised by how much I know from my nerdy podcasts and a bunch of the side reading I'd been doing.

And then a little idea pops into my head. An idea for the perfect paper.

CHAPTER 25

BECCA

In the end, I get a solid A on the paper.

As well as make up a few assignments I missed, which earns me partial credit.

Now there's just one thing left for me to do.

I find my purse, dig into the bottom. And there it is, nestled and wrinkly with bits of lint clumping into the folds. Pulling out the test to see what I missed is maybe the hardest part of coming back to myself.

I know that I don't *have* to look at it, don't have to figure out what I did wrong. After all, it's done. But I realize that I want to know what I did wrong. Screwing up isn't the most fun part of learning, but it's definitely got its hard-knock place on the learning curve.

My eyes move slowly down the paper. Multiple choice looks mostly good—a few errors where I didn't read through the question thoroughly. Careless, but not terrible. Short answer I nail. Which means…the three essays. They weren't just three essays, but three connected essays, building on each other. Which means that when you miss an essential building block, you kind of mess all of them up.

At first, I'm annoyed that the professor docked me each time—after all, he knew it was the same mistake, repeated a dozen times. But then I realize that the mistakes are a little like real science. Each piece has to be in its correct place, whether you're conducting an experiment or making a diagnosis or studying animal mating patterns.

I set the test down. And then I throw it away. I don't need it anymore. I know what I did wrong. I know what I can do right next time. It doesn't have to haunt me from the crevices of my bag. Looking at that helpless paper at the bottom of the trash feels oddly good. Like I looked fear in the face and fear—being the coward that it is—ran away.

Which means… I turn to my computer. My professor probably has all the grades in for what we've done so far. I shake my fingers, type in my password.

When I open it up, looking through the grades, I realize something else. He curved the midterm. Apparently, I wasn't the only one not nailing it. The curve hasn't skyrocketed me into excellence. But it did bring the grade up to a high C. C+. Average plus, I think, remembering Lance. Which means, I could maybe even get an A in the class.

And then I realize I'm getting a wee bit ahead of myself. After all, with my partial credits and that average plus, I still have a ways to go.

Still, with the information from that test in my brain, and the paper from the test in the garbage, I now know that I can do it.

At least if I keep up the momentum as I plow toward the final.

The truth is that I owe Lance a big thank you. Renting that room shook a lot of things out of me— the least of which was the compulsion to re-open my books, to re-look at what I'd started.

The greatest of which was to realize what had been missing inside of me. It wasn't a specific class or amount of time. It was the right, the ability to search for who I really was, and to be willing to go after her, regardless of what other people wanted me to do or be.

I'm not sure I'm ready to say that last part to

him, and still not sure who that girl is that I really want to be, but I know that she's in there somewhere, and that I have a right to be curious about who she is.

This week registration for fall semester begins. I'm going to sign up for three classes. Nine credit hours. Technically a full course load. The thought makes my heart beat a little faster.

It's been a week since I've seen Lance. I thought at first that he would text. Actually, I thought at first that I would text, but every time I pulled up my phone, I didn't know what to say.

I don't regret what I said or did in that hotel room, though maybe I could have been a little more graceful about it. And I can't say that I'm sure anymore that we're right for each other. It's seeming more and more like maybe we're not.

I mean, if he needs me to be that other person, well, I'm just not. And how do you say any of that in a text? You don't. You go talk to the person and tell him. Face to face.

Which is what I haven't have the courage to do. But now, with my aced paper, with my second shot, I know I've got to. To say thank you, if nothing else.

And I admit that I hope for something more than just thank you. I hope that we can patch up whatever got broken that night, hope that things can be right —truly right—between the two of us.

It's not till I ring his bell that I begin to wonder if he'll want to see me. I could offer to pay him back for the hotel room, but something about that feels so hollow I'm surprised I even thought it.

While I'm still trying to think of what to do, he opens the door. He's wearing his pajamas and looking wrinkled and it occurs to me that he was probably up all night saving lives, and might need to sleep sometime. I should have texted first.

"Oh, hey Becca," he says, like he doesn't hate my guts, but also didn't expect to see me here.

"I'm so sorry I woke you up."

"No biggie. I was needing to get up soon anyway. I hate to sleep the WHOLE day away."

"Can I come in?"

"It's kind of a mess."

That sounds like a no. "Well, I just wanted you to know that I really appreciated the hotel room, the kick in the pants. I, well, I used my time there as well as I could, and I pulled out a couple of decent grades in the class."

"That's great, Becca." Sincere, but cool. "I'm glad you're getting what you want."

"It's not that I'm getting it exactly," I say, trying to

get him to look into my eyes, to really see me. "It's that I'm figuring it out."

"That's great," he says. Again.

"I owe you a big thank you."

"Accepted," he replies. He looks at me smiling—big, sincere. But then the door is closing. Not slamming, just narrowing.

And it feels like we're done.

Which wasn't what I'd hoped for, and I want to say that, but don't know how. After all, what had I hoped for, exactly? I'd hoped for—I don't know—a hug maybe. I'd hoped he'd understand that what I want is multi-faceted, not just a class or a job or a family or a guy, but a full life with lots of all of those things. It still feels like he's wanting me to pick, or feeling like I did pick and he's not too happy about it.

He pauses just before the door closes all the way. I can see half of him still, looking at me. "And I guess I should tell you that you've inspired me as well," he says through the partially-open door.

I shoot him a confused look. "What do you mean?"

"I signed up for a class, too. Intro to law."

"Really?" I ask, because it seems like we both know it's the wrong choice.

"Security matters," he says.

"Happiness matters," I reply.

"Same thing," he answers, and the door is closing.

It all feels like slow motion, but I'm still not fast enough to stop it; in fact, I'm frozen. I don't even lift an arm.

When the door is closed and I'm just standing there alone, I whisper, "No, it's not."

But there's no one to counter me, to argue, to work through the sticky stuff.

No one at all.

It's 8:45, and I'm supposed to unlock the vet office at 9:00. So I do.

CHAPTER 26

LANCE

The weeks are flying by, the temperature dropping, the leaves changing. Which means that Maverick's next round of shots are coming up fast. I take her to PetStop. Victoria administers them with a quick precision and doesn't even notice that Maverick still has a small limp in her right foreleg.

That doesn't stop me from asking her to dinner.

We make it two dates this time before I can't do it anymore. I'm not quite sure what it is. Maybe that when I tell her about the law class, she orders a bottle of champagne and says, "That's something to celebrate."

I let her drink it all, and I'm pretty sure she doesn't notice that either.

For our third date, I tell her I've got the flu, and after that, I just don't call.

A month later, when fall is beginning and Maverick gets the worst case of fleas ever, I realize I've burned two vet clinics out of the ranks with my dating life.

Google is going to have to pick where I go this time. Unfortunately, Doctor Reynolds' clinic comes up at the top of the charts. She's got a bazillion five-star reviews too. PetStop, not nearly so many.

I settle on a place called Animal Village, but when I make the call, they tell me it'll cost an extra $100 for bringing in a new patient. I'm glad they can't see my face when I hang up.

"Do you really need flea medicine?" I ask Maverick. "I mean, we could order a generic one from the internet, right?"

She looks at me with her clear eye in a way that says, *Whatever you say, boss.* Then scratches her behind passionately.

I pull up my Amazon app to look for flea medicine and wonder if I should try going back to Dr. Reynolds' office. Which makes me think of Becca, which makes me wonder what she's studying.

Fall semester started just a few weeks ago. And with it, my faltering study of law.

I have a class tonight that I'm solidly planning on skipping. Not like Becca skipped, so she could be my Girl Friday or something. Nope. I just want to skip because I hate it. Every minute.

But even though I make big plans to not attend my class, a check arrives—delivered to me, not Mom —from my dad in the mail.

My dad. Sending me a check. Even though I'm a thirty-one-year-old homeowner with a full-time job. Still, it makes me feel guilty, childish. I grab my laptop and pull into the parking lot just as a Ford Taurus pulls up beside me. I know that car, and freeze in my own.

Becca gets out, dragging a bag full of papers and who knows what else. Even though I know she's my own age, she looks nineteen and I smile to myself, thinking that these guys probably hit on her all the time.

She turns back to her car, like she forgot something, and it's then that she sees me.

I can't hide, and it would be ridiculous and childish to just sit in my car and ignore her. I open the door and clamber out. "Hey, Becca."

"Lance!" she says and it sounds like real, authentic joy in her voice. Guess even she wants me in law school. "I never thought I'd see you here."

"Yeah, I told you I was taking that class."

"Oh, I know," she says. "But I just didn't know when it was, and...here you are." She gives me a once over, and I won't say I don't kind of like that. "You look nice," she says.

I can't quite remember what I'm wearing so I give myself a once over too. Red t-shirt, my favorite jeans. "You look great too," I say. And it's not just the blue shirt that matches her eyes, the tight black skinny jeans that show off those sleek calves. Those things are nice, but they were always there. But here, with that stupid heavy bag she's lugging, a glow has taken over her. It goes from her eyes to her smile all the way to her hair. "What classes are you taking this semester?" I ask, then laugh. "We sound like twenty-year-olds."

She laughs too. "Tell me about it. I don't feel like one, though. I had to go to a chiropractor about my shoulder last week."

"All those books," I say. Then second guess myself. Will she take it as a criticism? "Not that there's anything wrong with that?"

She laughs again. "For *real* though. The chiropractor recommended I buy a different bag. Just waiting for it to come in the mail. Okay, now I sound ninety years old instead of twenty."

I laugh and have this enormous urge to wrap her up in a hug. "But what classes?" I say instead.

"Oh, yeah," she says. "I'm taking chemistry and basic math, and the next anatomy class. But this stuff isn't exactly for a class."

She points to the enormous bag, and I realize she's gushing about it, the words tumbling out in a rush. "It's another research project. My professor was intrigued by one of my essay answers for the final. She asked me to work with her again. On this project about circulation. It's really cool."

"Whoa," I say. "Doesn't seem like community college stuff at all."

She laughs like I'm more clever than I am. "It's not exactly. For her, or for me. She's hoping to get some papers published and move up to a bigger college and I...well, I just love this stuff. Research," she says. "Papers. The whole thing. Who knew?"

She did, I realize.

Somewhere in her heart of hearts. That sweet curiosity that made her good at lots of things, that made her research Maverick's leg, that made her able to help her sister with the video editing.

It was all there all along.

"How's Maverick?" she asks, and I know that she

must realize I didn't bring her in for her vaccinations.

"She's great," I say. "The sweetest thing as always. I've started running with her in the mornings, and she's doing pretty well."

"The leg?" she asks.

"A little gimpy, but she makes do."

"Hmmm," Becca says, and I see the wheels turning. "I wasn't much help before. Let me talk to my professor and see if she's got any idea. Movement, it's totally her thing."

"And your class?" she asks.

"Yeah, good," I say. A lie.

"You like it?" she asks, moving closer, and I feel like I'm falling into some kind of trap.

"Sure, it's fine," I answer. "People need security."

"People need happiness," she answers in a way that feels like a correction. "To find what they love, to do what they're good at. That's what brings security."

So she's an evangelist now, is she? "Fine," I say, some sort of rebellious irritation creeping into me. "I hate it. I stink at it. I'm thinking of dropping the class."

"You should do what you love, Lance."

"I already do," I snap.

"I know," she says.

We both pause, like we're thinking that over.

"So you think I should drop the class, just fail."

"Would it be a failure?" she asks. "To experiment? To learn something about yourself?"

"Yes," I answer. "Obviously."

But is it obvious?

She looks at me. I look at her. A wildly irrational charge runs through me and I almost just sweep her up and kiss her. But that's definitely not what nice, rational lawyers do. "Well, I gotta go."

She reaches out, her fingers brushing mine, then pulls her hand back, worried she took a misstep. The warmth of her touch lingers, tingling along my fingertips, like it did the very first time, like it did every time.

"It's really good to see you," she says. "Thanks again for that hotel room. Thanks for saving *me*. You really are good at that."

CHAPTER 27

LANCE

That night when I show up for my shift, we get a call before I've even hung up my jacket.

Somebody's armed and suicidal. The police are trying to talk him down. That's the tough job.

Our job is to show up and wait, hoping they succeed. If they don't, well, then we get to step in and do what we do—try to save a life, even one that doesn't necessarily want to be saved.

We wait for an hour on scene. The man hides in the alley behind his apartment. The police have blocked off the area, talking to him through a megaphone. He weeps, then waves the gun around, staggers back to the brick wall.

Me, I have to pee. Like, exceptionally badly.

The scene is still slow, still stalled. I figure we've got another hour or two before anything happens. And I will NOT last that long.

I tell my partner I'm going to see if there's a lobby or something, and hop out of the ambulance, looking for a place that might be open, when I hear a shout, a whole series of them.

I turn to see the man raise his weapon, his mouth open in a gaping wail.

The police shoot him with beanbags—a tactic they sometimes use to get a person to stop, and then I feel it—sharp, searing, hot hot pain.

It knocks me back and I scream, though it's lost in all the other noise.

The man sinks to his knees as a bunch of cops rush to him—his gun has been thrown to the side.

My partner is hollering at me, but I can't hear the words; I'm holding my shoulder, the hot, red blood. The noises echo in my head, pulsing and rickety.

I know what's coming next, know it like my own name, but I can't stop it. The black creeps into my vision, then takes it over completely.

hen I wake up I'm in a white bed in a white room. I close my eyes to block out the whiteness, but when I do, I feel the throb of pain—pulsing with each beat of my heart. Groaning, I lean back into the hospital bed, then stab a button.

By the time the nurse arrives, I've checked my IV and heart monitor, and put several pieces of the puzzle together.

"Awake at last," she says like I'm five and it's my birthday.

"Yippee," I reply.

"Rough night at work," she says, glancing at her clipboard. This nurse is vaguely familiar to me, though I can't find a name right now, which means I'm probably on some pain meds.

"Can't actually say I've had worse," I reply. "I've put together a few basic details, but would you mind filling me in on the rest?"

"You got shot," she says.

"Yup. Figured that part out. Shoulder," I say. "Or side." I look sideways, trying to see.

"Correct. Just below your shoulder. But nothing major got hit, which is good news. The muscle and skin will need to heal, but no bones, arteries, major nerves. Congratulations."

"But how, exactly, did I get shot?"

"You'll have to talk to your guys about that," she says.

Right on cue, I hear the bustle in the hall. Jordan's voice first, followed by several of the cops. They bring in—I'm not kidding—balloons. "Got these at Walmart," Jordan says, laughing. "They're a dollar a piece. Sweet deal, huh?"

"Makes me feel like a princess," I reply. "Now tell me why I got shot."

One of the cops jumps in. "We got the guy to drop his gun, but he didn't drop it; he kind of tossed it."

I nod, a bit of comprehension dawning. "But the safety wasn't on."

"And you'd gotten out of the ambulance, for who knows why," another cop says.

"I had to pee, dude. You guys were taking forever."

"Scene safety," he clucks, and they all laugh, but it's kind of a nervous thing.

I really shouldn't have gotten out, could even get in trouble for being a little reckless and getting myself shot. But the guys are laughing again, so I push the thought away.

"And then we were running for the guy," a cop is saying. "And Jordan here was hollering at you to grab the equipment bag, but then he glanced over at you."

"And you just sank down," Jordan says. "Like a dead faint, and I know a damsel in distress when I see one."

"Thanks, man," I say, laughing, then hurting.

"So I'm running to you, and these guys are running to the guy who was supposed to be the patient. And it was just total chaos."

"That dude doing okay?" I ask. "Probably doesn't help to be suicidal and then realize you shot somebody else."

"Doubt he knows," one of the cops says.

"That's for the best," I reply.

"Fire department was on scene, so—you know—they saved the day."

"Like they do," I reply.

"When you've got the sexiest calendars, you're always the hero," Jordan says.

"Tell me about it, man," I say, settling back. "When they gonna make an EMS calendar?"

"Probably when I get less fat," Jordan says, poking at his gut.

"Yeah, you gotta get on that," I say, then, "Hey, thanks."

"Anytime. Truth is you did me a favor. I got to sleep a couple hours at the station while they looked for someone to come in for you."

"Sweet," I say.

"Yup. Made it till almost four when Callen arrived."

"Callen?" I ask. "He's off leave?"

"He is now," Jordan said. "I talked him into it. Told him it was for you. He'll be here later today, by the way, for a visit."

"Well, I'll be darned," I murmur.

"Silver lining and all," Jordan says. "But anyway, when Callen came in, we got a pooper. It was all over the bed, man. You should have seen. Home health didn't show up, or something. I think the smell burned out all the hairs in my nose. Callen almost puked."

"Ugh," I answer. "Good night to get shot."

"You couldn't have picked a better one," Jordan says.

"You tell your wife you're getting home late this morning?" I ask.

"Yeah," he says. "I said you went and got yourself shot. She's making you breakfast."

"You're kidding."

"You know I'm not."

Thirty minutes later, Jordan's wife, Emily, is there with biscuits, gravy, fat sweet blueberries, and some kind of mocha hot chocolate. "When you gonna leave Jordan and marry me?" I ask her.

Jordan laughs and Emily asks where that pretty little girl is that I was dating.

"Probably in class," I say. And then I remember—Maverick. She's going to be worried, needs to be let out. I groan.

"What?" Jordan asks, yawning.

"My dog," I say. "She's going to need food, and a potty break." I glance at the wall clock. "Hopefully she hasn't pooped on the floor yet."

"I'll head over there, man," Jordan says. "You know where your keys are?" He's yawning again. Twelve long hours. A code brown for his last call, the call after his partner got shot and then fainted.

"You know what," I say, looking around for my phone. "Don't worry about it. I've got a friend who can do it."

"Hope it's that girl," Emily says.

How do women do that, know that stuff? "It's just a friend," I say.

She clucks, and I text Becca.

Becca knows where I hide the emergency key, I tell myself. She's the only logical choice. "Hey. This is kind of a crazy favor, but I got a little hurt at work. Could you let Maverick out this morning before you go to work?"

She texts right back. "Sure. You okay?"

"Yeah," I text, glancing at my bandaged shoulder. "Just a few stitches and stuff."

"So sorry. No worries. I'll let Maverick out. Maybe even take her to work with me. She's got to be due for her final round of shots soon."

Again, how do women do this? If I didn't have my phone, I wouldn't remember anything about anyone's shots. And it's not even Becca's dog—how did she remember?

"You don't have to," I text. "Just make sure she's got food and water and can do her business."

Somehow I know she's not going to listen. I know she's going to take her to work, check her charts, baby her.

"Good," Jordan's wife is saying, glancing over my shoulder. "Glad it's her."

"Emily," I say. "You know we broke up, right?"

"What I don't know is why," she says, puttering around and cleaning up the crumbs from my breakfast. "You two deserve each other, so whatever you messed up, you go on and fix it."

"I tried," I say. "She's just too smart for me."

"Well, maybe she isn't going and getting herself shot, but otherwise I don't believe that for a second."

I want to argue, but Jordan's fallen asleep on the chair and my own eyes are drooping. "Don't let him drive home," I mutter.

She pats my cheek, just like a grandmother would.

And then I'm alone with my white bed and white walls, my IV and pulse oximeter, and that sweet, sweet pain drip.

The sun is dropping down when I wake up again. And someone is sitting by my bed. I assume it's that nurse, the one whose name I can't remember. She puts a soft hand against my cheek and I want to lean into those warm fingers, but I know she's married. "I have to go to the bathroom," I murmur before turning my head, before seeing the halo of wavy hair, before hearing the soft snort of laughter.

"I'll call the nurse," Becca says, "but they might have you hooked up to a catheter."

I blink, not sure if I'm actually awake.

"You didn't tell me you had stitches because you got *shot*," she says.

"Details," I murmur, looking around. "Is Maverick here?"

"In the car," she answers. "They wouldn't let me bring her in."

"But you're here," I say, and take her hand. Part of me is yelling at me to stop, but the other part of me is way way too drugged to listen.

"I went back to your apartment after work, expecting to see you there, to give my report on how well Maverick did today at the office, to see whatever part of you had gotten stitches. But you weren't there. And it was clear you hadn't been all day."

Through the fog of my meds, I try to remember what state my apartment was in when I went to work yesterday. Maybe not the best state ever.

"I wasn't sure what to do, so I called your work, thinking maybe I'd kept her too long and you'd had to go in. I figured I'd take her home with me if that was the case. Turned out, you'd never come home." She gives me a look like a mother scolding a child, but she hasn't let go of my hand and is, in fact, stroking the fingers. I let my mind sink into those warm tingles.

"Maverick did well with her shots?" I ask.

"Of course," she says, then kind of giggles. "Shots. The irony. Want to tell me what happened?"

I slur parts of the story and might have fallen asleep at one point, but by the time my dinner arrives, I've got it all out and they've adjusted my pain meds down a bit and I'm feeling kind of alright, albeit a little embarrassed. "It's Wednesday," I say suddenly.

"Yeah," she replies.

"You have class. Or research, or whatever it was."

"I do," she says, "but I told my professor that I had an emergency, and that my paramedic friend had gotten *shot*. You have class too," she says.

"Ah, another advantage to getting shot," I say with a smile.

"You like your class that much, huh?"

"I hate it," I answer, and clearly the drugs aren't completely worn off because I'm like a drunk dude spilling all his secrets. "That time you saw me, I hadn't been in weeks. But you love yours. Why aren't you there?"

"Lance," she says, drawing out my name. "You. Got. Shot."

"But your class is important to you," I say, my brain feeling sleek and slippery.

"Yes," she asks. "But other things are important too. And sometimes they're even more important."

"How'd Maverick do?" I ask, repeating myself and sort of knowing that through the fog, but sort of not.

"She did great," Becca says, leaning forward so that her face is really close to mine. "You did too. I'm coming back tomorrow. Maybe with your mother. I took the day off work."

"You didn't have to do that," I say.

"No," she answered. "I didn't. But I want to. And I hope you want me here."

"Yup," I say, my eyelids drooping again. "I want you every day."

She smiles. I see it as I drift off. Something soft brushes my cheek, and then I'm sinking into my dreams, my soft-fingered, sweet dreams.

CHAPTER 28

LANCE

*O*ne advantage of getting shot: it makes it a whole lot easier to drop a class you hate, a whole lot easier to explain it to the teacher and get away without a lot of follow-up questions about all the classes I skipped before getting shot, a whole lot easier to write my dad and tell him to stop sending the checks for classes I never wanted to take anyway.

Though not a whole lot easier to explain to him why you want to keep the job that you love, that you're good at, but that just got you shot.

For now, I don't worry about that part, though I'll need to in the future. Because the truth is that I never want the checks again, never plan to become a lawyer, and just want to be allowed to do my thing without a bribe.

Another advantage of getting shot is that Becca comes over every night. Even after I'm released from the hospital, especially after I'm released from the hospital.

At 6:13 on the dot, she arrives to let Maverick out and take her for a walk. Then she fixes me a quick meal—I tell her she doesn't have to every time, but she does anyway. Then she either goes to her class, or settles in beside me in the living room to read though loads of textbooks and articles about circulation. Sometimes she talks about them.

If you'd asked me if I thought the topic of the circulatory system was interesting, I'd have thought you were joking with the question, because who even asks such a thing? But when Becca talks about it, all enthusiasm and interest, she brings out all the little details and nuances that make these things cool; and suddenly circulation *is* interesting. It might be extra interesting when you've just been shot.

"See," she says, tracing the lines of veins along my shoulder. "You're so, so lucky; it didn't hit the subclavian artery." With her tracing my healing shoulder, I definitely feel lucky.

"Maybe you should be a high school teacher," I tell her one night. "I might have paid more attention."

She laughs. "I thought about that too. I do like talking about it, but one of my friends said that teachers have a really limited curriculum—they've got to teach what the state wants them to teach and to stick to it pretty solidly. And I guess I'm a bit over sticking to things other people want me to do."

I put my good arm over her shoulders. "Thank you," I whisper in her ear.

"For what?" she says, like she's not in my house, taking care of me.

"For saving *me*."

"I didn't do that," she says. "Your partner did, and the nurses and doctors at the hospital."

"I was trying to be romantic," I groan. "But seriously. Thank you for helping me get better, for taking care of Maverick, for making me meals. You really don't have to."

"I want to," she answers. "It's what friends do."

"Friends," I reply.

"People who care about each other."

"Which could still be friends," I say.

"Or maybe more than that," she adds, looking into my eyes.

"Yes," I say. "Or more than that."

I touch her chin. "You helped me to see who I

was and what I wanted. I shouldn't have needed help, but I did."

"Now you're just being cheesy."

"Yeah," I say. "I am. You don't have to be here right now. Even if you were helping me—and Maverick." My dog wags her tail at the sound of her name. "And the last time you were here a lot, it wasn't really right."

"That's because I was here being someone who wasn't really me."

"And you're not anymore?" I ask.

"I'm not," she says. "Right now. This. It's exactly where I want to be, exactly what I want to be doing. Talking to you, taking that crazy dog for a walk, and studying. It's the perfect life."

"Is it?" I ask.

She looks at me, hears the seriousness of my tone. For a moment, she closes her eyes. I reach out and take her hand. At first, she doesn't respond. Her hand just lies there. Then she takes a deep breath and wraps her fingers through mine. All that glorious soft tingling. "It's my best life."

"Well then, maybe we should make more of it," I say, leaning toward her.

"Maybe we already are," she responds, running her fingers through my hair-that-needs-a-cut, and pulling me even closer toward her. We hover there for just a moment, eyes closing, cheeks flushing, and then a kiss. Not a first kiss. Not a new kiss.

Better than that.

A kiss that knows the contours of the others' lips. A kiss that knows the way her head tips to the side. A kiss that finds the sweetest points of her mouth and face. But also, a kiss that goes deeper than skin.

A kiss that understands the heart that beats underneath, a kiss that hears the goals and dreams and insecurities and sacrifices. A kiss that accepts the weaknesses and irritations.

A kiss that knows. And loves.

Better than any kiss I've ever had before.

I pull her body toward mine—not too hard—I've still got several stitches in my shoulder. But stitches won't last forever.

When we finally break apart, I ask her, "What can I do for you? I don't want you to just be here playing nurse."

"I like playing nurse," she says.

"Really?" I ask coyly. "I could buy you a sexy costume. That could be my contribution."

"Maybe keep brainstorming," she replies. "Or you could help me study."

"You mean we get to play doctor."

"You wish. We get to play physical therapist."

"I can work with that," I say, then glance at her laptop. "What are we working on today?"

"Okay, so when we're injured, the body sends a certain amount of inflammation to the wound. In fact, inflammation gets a bad rap, because without it the systems of the body would never be able to heal. But anyway, I'm wondering if it would speed your recovery if we bring heat to the shoulder with a heating pad or something. That would stimulate circulation at the place of the injury, and I'm guessing your wound would love all that fresh, yummy oxygen-rich blood."

"You're guessing?" I ask.

"Well, not too much. Heat does bring fresh blood to the site."

"I think you're using me as a human experiment."

"Oh, I've only just begun," she says.

"Are you sure you don't want to just be a sexy nurse?"

"Definitely not," she answers. "If anything, I'm going to have to be a sexy mad scientist. Now where do you keep your heating pads?"

"Bathroom, beneath the sink," I say. "But you know you don't have a control group or anything. How will you know if it works?"

She pops that eyebrow. I love it when she does that.

"So you do know a thing or two about this stuff." She walks down the hall to the bathroom, and I can hear her digging around.

"I like science," I say when she gets back and plugs in the heating pad. "Just not law. So you don't think it will bring too much blood to the fresh wound?" I ask.

"Only one way to find out."

"You are mad."

"Not too much," she says. "We'll stop the experiment if there's excessive distress to the patient."

"Are you sure I can't be the control group?"

"Cowboy up, Lance," she mock-scolds me, sitting down and patting the couch beside her. "And it will be a little circumstantial, but still fairly interesting."

"I'm not complaining," I say, leaning over so I'm splayed onto her lap. "Heal me."

She sighs in a theatrical sort of way, then pokes playfully at a spot close to my wound.

"Ouch," I say, swatting her hand. "That's not what you were supposed to do."

"Science," she says with an exceptionally prim look.

"I can think of a few more interesting ways we can study."

"This is interesting," she says, examining the area around my shoulder for real now. "And, seriously, if this doesn't feel good, let me know." She gently places the heating pad over my dressings.

I gaze at her, hair falling over her shoulders, cheeks flushed with interest. What can I say? It *is* interesting. Out of the blue, I blurt, "There's not a lot of money in it, the things I do."

She looks at me like I'm speaking gibberish.

"It's something my dad is always saying," I add.

"You don't need money," she says. "Just to love what you do."

"Well, you need a little money," I say.

"You have a little money," she says, gesturing around at my house. "Plenty of money."

"But you know romance novels," I say. "The guy is always loaded. Or becomes loaded. Doing what I do, I'm never going to become loaded."

"Well, lucky for us, I don't read romance novels," she replies. "Only anatomy books. And you're doing just fine in that department."

"Tell me more," I say, reaching up to trace her lips with my finger as she finally glances away from my shoulder. She looks down at me, my head propped on her lap. I reach up, touch her cheek. "But also, I'm serious. Is it enough?"

"You're competent, smart, brave, kind. And good-looking of course." She takes one of my hands and moves it to her lips, giving it a soft kiss. "But to be even more serious. You can take care of people, all kinds of people—those who desperately need it and those who definitely don't—two very different skill sets. You help heal people, help calm people. You deal on a daily basis with things most of us could hardly deal with on a yearly basis. You save, but you also stand by when people can't be saved and witness for that, for the passing of that life. So, yes, I think it's enough."

I push myself up out of her lap so I can really look into her face.

"All this time I've been jealous of you, Lance," she continues. "That you really knew what it was that made you tick, and that you were good at, too. While I was floundering around like a freshman in college. Which I technically am, but that's not what I mean. I'm thirty-one years old and didn't know what I wanted to do with my life."

I laugh, put a hand to her waist.

"You have money," she says. "We both do. Why would we even want to be romance-novel rich—it'd probably just make us jerks or something? What we need is more than that, bigger than that. I think I'm finding it with school. And with you."

She looks at me. "And I think you already knew what you wanted, and what you needed."

"I did," I say. "I've known for a while what I was good at, what made me tick. So I guess I needed something different than you did. I needed to understand that the thing I love was okay, was enough."

"Definitely enough," she says.

"But I needed something else, too. Or I wanted something else."

"And what is that?" she asks.

"Someone to share it with, to hear the stories, to be okay with this slightly weird life."

"We all have weird lives, Lance." She runs a thumb over my cheekbone, and I close my eyes, feeling the magnet of our bodies. When our lips meet again, hers are full and wet and soft, her cheeks flushed with the fever of the moment.

She pulls away laughing, then fans her face. "You *are* good at what you do."

"I would say that you're not so bad at it either, but I wouldn't want you to think I wasn't taking you seriously as a person."

"Oh, stop," she says. "We all know boss scientist girls can be cute, too."

"I suppose…" I murmur, and then she's wrapping her arms around my neck again. We're lost in the heat of our mouths and bodies, the press and pull of the moment, the pleasure at the simple beauty of it all.

Until something cool nudges my arm and I jump, which hurts my shoulder. Maverick is gazing into my eyes.

"Guess she was worried we'd forget her w-a-l-k," Becca says.

She wags her tail, whines as she looks at the door.

"Great, she's learned to spell," Becca grumbles.

"I always knew she was smart," I say.

Becca's lacing up her shoes. "I'll take her out really quick, let her do her business."

"I'll come too," I say. "Though I won't do any business at this juncture."

"Now that's romantic," she says, hooking Maverick's leash up to her collar. "Are you sure you're feeling up to it?"

"I'll be back at work in several weeks. I hope I can help walk my own dog."

"Competent," she says. "Like I said."

"And hot," I add. "You said that too."

"The hottest," she adds. "Guess you've got to have something going for you if you're not a billionaire."

"Well, I try to do my part," I say.

"But more than hot," she says, smiling and taking my hand. "Much more."

A lot like this is more than a moment; it's one in a series of moments that make us *us.*

I lean down to steal one more kiss, just as Maverick starts to piddle on the floor.

"Out out out," we both yell, and she leaves a little trickle of a pee trail—most of it fortunately outside of my condo.

"This means we're ready for a committed relationship, right?" I ask. "When we can stop making out long enough to take the dog out."

"You mean, 'almost' stop 'almost' in time to take the dog out."

"Almosts are part of a committed relationship, right?"

"I guess they are," she says, winding her fingers through mine. "Almosts are part of figuring it all out."

"Do I have to wear makeup?" I ask Sally Mae as she fusses over the collar of my shirt, smoothing wrinkles.

"Only if you want to," she says.

"Well, in that case," I reply.

She pops an eyebrow, and all of a sudden I see the resemblance between the two sisters.

"Nervous?" she asks.

"A little," I say.

She bends over Maverick, cooing, and adjusting her purple collar to just the right angle. "What a beautiful baby," she says.

Maverick wags her tail in response, the newly adjusted collar slipping just a little so the buckle is now slightly off center. That's my girl.

Maverick, for the record, is not the least bit nervous.

To the side of the recording studio, I see Becca standing in the doorway, going over the notes. "You didn't include the part at the end about him ripping off his shirt and flexing as he holds Maverick to his chest," she says, her nose in the paper.

"Yeah, we had to cut that part," Sally deadpans right back at her. "The firefighter calendar was threatening to sue for rights infringement."

"Yeah, you can't have EMS looking *too* hot," Becca says, nose still in the notes.

"Ouch," I say, as Sally Mae clips a little microphone to my shirt.

"Besides, we needed a place to put the mic," she says.

"Don't be nervous," Becca says from her spot in the doorway.

"It's my first celebrity debut," I say. "How can I not be nervous?"

Both of the sisters laugh.

"For real, though," Sally says. "We'll edit out anything awkward and by the end it'll be smooth as butter."

"I'm editing the shirt off too," Becca says. "Hope your chest is smooth as butter, Lance."

"Great, now we've got a running gag," I say.

"Oh, don't pretend this gag wasn't running before," she answers.

"You ready?" Sally asks.

"As I'll ever be," I answer.

Becca clicks the lights on. Sally gestures to the couch, where I sit, and Maverick flops casually like she was made for the movies.

"Today we're interviewing paramedic Lance Patterson and his dog, Maverick. Tell us about yourself, Lance."

And I do. It's not the most graceful thing in the world, but after a sentence or two, Maverick plants her head on my lap, ears flopping, in the sweetest way imaginable.

"If I understand correctly," Sally is saying. "You recently found Maverick on a call."

"Well, after," I reply. "She was at the scene. And injured. I figured I'd help her out and then help her find her home. But she didn't have one."

"She does now," Sally says, leaning forward to lace one of Maverick's soft ears through her fingers.

"She does," I say.

"But the story doesn't end there." Sally is looking at the camera, smiling, her cheeks bright and happy. "Lance might have saved Maverick, but in that way dogs so often do, she got the chance to save him back."

From the darkness in the corner, Becca winks.

"Yes," I say, clearing my throat. "Because recently when *I* was injured on a call, Maverick was there for me, helping me recover."

"Tell us about the injury."

Sally leans back and I go through the details, the hospital stay, the friends helping out. And Maverick. Getting me out of bed, insisting on her walks, standing nose to nose while I did my physical therapy sessions on the floor.

"Sounds like you got a few kisses while you were down there."

Right on cue, Maverick lifts her head off my lap to gaze into my eyes and lick my face.

We all laugh.

"It was enough to make my girlfriend jealous," I quip, winking at the camera.

Maverick positions herself completely on my lap.

And from the way Sally is laughing, I can tell that the interview is a success, and that Maverick is well on her way to her apparent dream of celebrity. Even she has found her calling. Who knew she was such a ham?

From the corner of the room, I steal another

glance at Becca. Even though she's standing in the literal shadows, her face is glowing as she watches her sister do what she loves, as she watches me talk about what I love.

Becca catches my eye, puts her palm up to her mouth, and then blows me a kiss.

A kiss that knows me, just as much as I know her.

ALSO BY J. E. PACE

From Ashes

From Gunpowder

Pulse: A Paramedic's Walk Along the Lines of Life and Death (a nonfiction collection of essays about the life of a paramedic)

Sign up for my NEWSLETTER and receive the short story, "Ready," for FREE!

Thanking the people who have helped is one of the best parts of writing a book. After all, putting a book together is a big event.

Thank you to my ARC readers and to my wonderful editor, Carrie.

I suppose this time around I have to thank my cat for making my TikTok account something people bother to look at.

Thank you, sweet readers for reading, reviewing, and supporting me.

A huge thank you to my husband who, in addition to being a huge supporter, is also a real-life paramedic. He gave me advice and suggestions on the scenes where actual medical knowledge was involved. (Any mistakes in the way EMS is portrayed in the book are due to me not asking enough questions. I'm hoping I did right in my portrayal of this important work.)

And, as always, a huge thank you to my family,

for supporting me in my creative endeavors, for reading my stuff, and for telling me I can do it when I just want to hide under the bed and cry (which I usually manage to avoid).

J. E. Pace is the author of the books *From Ashes, From Gunpowder,* and the short story "Ready," which you can get for free by signing up for her newsletter.

If you enjoy fantasy or memoir, you can find more of her work, written under the name Jean Knight Pace.

Or check out her website: jeanknightpace.com

www.ingramcontent.com/pod-product-compliance
Lightning Source LLC
Chambersburg PA
CBHW060920190726
48286CB00002B/580